Blaze

Dear Reader,

November is one of my favorite months of the year here in the South. Summer clings determinedly through the bulk of October, so November really ushers in our fall. The leaves turn, the breeze gets crisp and my husband and I are often on our deck in front the chimenea, warming our feet by a fire. We get to enjoy Thanksgiving without the rush of the Christmas holidays. And it's a great time to curl up with a good book, isn't it? (Hint, hint, nudge, nudge.)

When Lex Sanborn comes out of the military and goes to work for Ranger Security, the last thing he expects is to be paired up with Bess Cantrell, on the hunt for one of the few remaining "Wicked" Bibles. A printing error in the 1600s edition, which says, "Thou shalt commit adultery," makes this particular Bible one of the most valuable books on the market. And the forced proximity with the sexy "picker" is most definitely keeping sinning at the forefront of his mind.

Nothing brings a smile to my face faster than hearing from my readers, so be sure to check out my website at www.ReadRhondaNelson.com. Also, the Blaze Authors have taken on a Pet Project. Be sure to visit www.blazeauthors.com to see what we're up to and how you can help.

Happy reading!

Rhonda

Rhonda Nelson

THE SURVIVOR

™ **Harlequin**®

TORONTO NEW YORK LONDON
AMSTERDAM PARIS SYDNEY HAMBURG
STOCKHOLM ATHENS TOKYO MILAN MADRID
PRAGUE WARSAW BUDAPEST AUCKLAND

Recycling programs
for this product may
not exist in your area.

ISBN-13: 978-0-373-79649-6

THE SURVIVOR

Printed in U.S.A.

ABOUT THE AUTHOR

A Waldenbooks bestselling author, two-time RITA® Award nominee and *RT Book Reviews* Reviewers' Choice nominee, Rhonda Nelson writes hot romantic comedy for the Harlequin Blaze line and other Harlequin imprints. With more than twenty-five published books to her credit and many more coming down the pike, she's thrilled with her career and enjoys dreaming up her characters and manipulating the worlds they live in. In addition to a writing career, she has a husband, two adorable kids, a black Lab and a beautiful bichon frise. She and her family make their chaotic but happy home in a small town in northern Alabama. She loves to hear from her readers, so be sure and check her out at www.readrhondanelson.com.

Books by Rhonda Nelson

HARLEQUIN BLAZE
255—THE PLAYER
277—THE SPECIALIST
283—THE MAVERICK
322—THE EX-GIRLFRIENDS' CLUB
361—FEELING THE HEAT
400—THE LONER
412—THE HELL-RAISER
475—LETTERS FROM HOME
481—THE SOLDIER
545—THE RANGER
549—BORN ON THE 4TH OF JULY
    "The Prodigal"
557—THE RENEGADE
579—IT MUST HAVE BEEN THE MISTLETOE...
    "Cole for Christmas"
586—THE REBEL
594—THE WILD CARD
615—REAL MEN WEAR PLAID

For Beverly. I miss you.

Prologue

LEX SANBORN HAD NEVER wondered what his last thoughts before dying would be, but he certainly hadn't expected an intense craving for pineapple sherbet and having lines from American poet Alan Seeger's *I Have a Rendezvous with Death* running through his mind.

I have a rendezvous with Death, at some disputed barricade, when Spring comes back with rustling shade, and apple blossoms fill the air...

The initial pain from the hit had receded, leaving a contented warmth in most of his body, an odd coldness at the site of the wound. His shoulder, he knew, more from the remembered pain of the injury and the absence of any real feeling now. Though he couldn't open his eyes, he could hear them working above him, knew they were doing everything they could, and a part of him wanted to tell them to stop, to save someone who wasn't going to die, that their efforts were wasted on him. He was finished. He could feel himself sliding further and further away, feel the blood leaving his body. Must have hit an artery...

But I've a rendezvous with Death, at midnight in some flaming town, when Spring trips north again this year...

"Lex! Lex, damn you, can you hear me?" Jeb, his best friend and fellow soldier, shouted near his ear.

He could, but as much as he wanted to, he couldn't respond. Couldn't do anything but drift away. He could feel himself getting smaller and smaller, shrinking into nothingness, and the nothingness felt wonderful, better than anything he'd ever felt before. A glow of euphoria started in his center and spread, his limbs going weightless. If he could have smiled, he would.

And I to my pledged word am true, I shall not fail that rendezvous.

1

Six months later...

FORMER RANGER TURNED newly minted security agent Lex Sanborn looked at the photocopied page of the Bible he'd been handed and felt his eyes widen in shock. "Thou *shalt* commit adultery?" Granted, he hadn't been to church in years, but he certainly didn't remember learning *this* particular version in Sunday school class.

Brian Payne, Jamie Flanagan and Guy McCann, owners of the elite security company who'd just hired him, all chuckled, presumably at his slack-jawed expression.

"That's why it's called the 'Wicked Bible,'" Payne explained. "This version was printed—accidentally, of course—in 1636 and there are only believed to be eleven surviving copies in the world. The New

York Public Library has one in its rare books section, there's another in Branson, Missouri, at the Bible museum, and the British Library actually had it on display, opened to the page of the misprint, during part of '09.'"

"It's very valuable," Jamie chimed in. Sprawled in a leather recliner with a sports drink in his hand, he was affable and easygoing and Lex had liked him instantly. Had taken an immediate liking to all of them actually.

Jamie Flanagan had been the original player until he met and married Colonel Garrett's granddaughter and purportedly sported a genius-level IQ. That quick brain combined with a substantial amount of brawn made him a force to be reckoned with. And with a lucky streak that bordered on the divine, Guy McCann's ability to skate the thin line between recklessness and perfection was still locker-room lore.

Known in certain circles as the Specialist, Brian Payne was coolly efficient and had strategy down to an art form. With an unmatched attention to detail, there was no such thing as half-assed in his world. He didn't tolerate it.

He was damned lucky to have a job here, Lex thought, thankful again to Colonel Carl Garrett for the recommendation. Was this what he'd imagined he'd be doing for the rest of his life? No. But six months ago he'd thought his life was over and that significantly changed things. Had changed him in ways that he wasn't altogether proud of, in ways he'd never, ever anticipated.

"It's worth around a hundred grand in today's market," Guy remarked.

Lex whistled low. Now it was beginning to make sense. He looked again at the picture Payne had handed him and searched the image for clues. The snapshot depicted an old Coca-Cola sign that had been propped up on a dusty counter covered with lots of other junk. A blue mason jar with a rusty lid, wooden spools, an old teakettle and— Ah, he thought, spying the black spine of the Wicked Bible just below the teakettle.

"So this is it? This is what they're after?"

"Yes," Payne told him. "At least, we think so. Bess came to see me yesterday and brought that with her. She said she'd gotten a few emails about the picture, but not the sign, which was what she had for sale. She's got an online store as well as the brick-and-mortar kind," he explained. "She says the emailer wanted to know where the picture was taken and that she wouldn't have told them regardless, but she genuinely didn't remember."

"She's a junk dealer?" he asked.

Payne almost smiled and a flash of humor momentarily lit his gaze. "She rescues antiques," he corrected, then gestured to a pair of old glass gas pumps in the corner. "For instance, I bought those from her. She has a great eye for things that are different. I've known her for years." His grin widened. "And for what it's worth, I wouldn't ever call her that to her face."

Lex nodded, appreciating the advice. If he was going to have to work with this old woman, then he didn't want to piss her off. In his limited experience, mostly with his grandparents, older folks were funny about their stuff. If he was reading this correctly, based on Payne's advice, Bess Cantrell was the same way.

"At any rate, she didn't hear from the emailer again and had chalked it up to an odd occurrence, nothing more," Payne continued. "Then night before last her store was broken into and the external hard drive to her computer was stolen. While the police were still there doing the report, Bess got a call from one of her clients, Walker Wiggins, who said a man had come to see him about a book—"

"The one in the picture obviously," Lex said, nodding grimly.

"—and that when he'd refused to let the man search his property, the stranger had gotten violent and tried to push past him into his house. His dog came to his rescue and ultimately sent the man packing, but Walker was shaken and concerned all the same."

Heartened to hear that the man had an animal willing to protect him—he adored dogs and had briefly considered going into veterinary school before joining the military—Lex nevertheless frowned. "Why had he called Bess to tell her all of this?"

"Because the man had told Walker that he was a friend of Bess's and had gotten his address from her." He shrugged. "Walker knew Bess better than that and called her to give her a heads-up. Since then, three other clients have been contacted in this manner, and on this last occasion, one was actually hurt."

Lex's blood boiled. So whoever this jackass was, he was dangerous *and* he was a bully. Bastard, Lex thought. No doubt the majority of Bess's clients were her age and older and they were being harassed and manhandled in their own homes over something that was, if they even had it, *theirs*.

"Naturally, Bess doesn't want anyone to get hurt, particularly any of her clients, and doesn't think that the police are going to truly be able to help her in time to prevent either a theft or a tragedy—" he grimaced "—or possibly both, unfortunately."

"So that's where you come in," Flanagan told him. "We're going to put a man at her store as a safety measure and you and Bess are going to go on the road and try to (a.) catch this guy and (b.) get to the book before he does. Obviously whoever has the book doesn't realize what it's worth. This person, whoever he is, no doubt is banking on that."

Lex nodded, certain that he could handle this. He only hoped that Bess didn't slow him down. He knew there were a lot of spry older people, ones who walked daily and kept themselves in shape, and he sincerely hoped that Bess Cantrell had done the same. If not, then he could easily see this becoming a problem. He inwardly grimaced. If she had a small bladder or a bad hip, they were going to be in serious trouble.

Honestly, he didn't see any good reason why Bess had to go along. He would be able to move faster without her and, so long as he had a list of her clients and a good map, he could take care of everything himself. After a moment, he said as much. "Look, I appreciate that Mrs. Cantrell wants to look after—"

"It's Miss," Payne corrected mildly. "She's not married."

A spinster then. Whatever. "—her clients," he continued. "But is there any particular reason why I can't do this without her?"

Jamie Flanagan and Guy McCann shared a brief look and McCann was obviously trying to keep from smiling. For whatever reason, Lex knew that anything that would make the irreverent McCann want to grin couldn't be anything that would work in Lex's favor. He studied all three of them again and knew that they were sharing some sort of private joke.

And it was at his expense.

Excellent.

"You can't do it without her because she's not going to let you," Payne said, releasing a long sigh. "These are her clients and she's the one who has inadvertently put them at risk. Also, a lot of these people aren't going to trust anyone but her, and if you show up without her, you're not any more credible than the other guy. Much as I'm sure you don't think so now, it's better that she goes with you."

Lex nodded, resigned. What choice did he have really? This was his first assignment and he was accustomed to taking orders. These weren't orders, exactly, but they might as well be, and he had no intention of rocking the boat.

Honestly, when the doctor had told him he was never going to get a full range of motion back in his shoulder and that there wasn't going to be any way he could continue with his unit, he'd been equally devastated and relieved. How two such opposing reactions could take place in the same body was simply amazing to him, but he had felt them both all the same. Devastated that his career was over, relieved because, for the first time in his life, to his absolute shame...he was afraid of dying. Afraid that that selfsame fear would prevent him from acting, from doing what needed to be done.

And a fearful soldier might as well be a dead one.

Born into a service-oriented family, Lex had been raised with the belief that every human being needed to leave the world a better place than they found it. His father had served in the army for twenty years, then went on to become a police officer. His mother was a retired schoolteacher who helped inmates at the local jail who didn't have their general education diplomas—GEDs—to get them so that they could apply for further continuing education classes. His brother was a medic, currently serving with the air force in Afghanistan, and his sister was a nurse.

His entire family contributed to the greater good of the world and he was unbelievably proud of them. They each had a purpose and, even though he'd had one up until six months ago, he'd never truly felt like his feet had been on the right path. He'd loved the military, had a tremendous regard for the men and women who served, and he'd been proud to be a part of it. But he'd always had the nagging suspicion that it wasn't what he was meant to do, to be.

Truthfully, he couldn't say being a security expert was what he wanted, either, but at least he was out of the military and would have time to pursue other interests.

He would be lying if he said there wasn't a hor-

Honey the dog

rible sense of guilt at leaving. He had friends over there on the front lines—most specifically Jeb Anderson, whom he'd gone through ROTC with—and coming home, out of the line of fire, felt wrong in a way that he couldn't accurately describe.

And the horrible part? The part that made him sick to his stomach with guilt, regret and shame?

He was glad to be home. Thankful to be out of the line of fire.

He'd had nightmares the first few months after he'd taken the hit—*hits* actually, four right into his shoulder, shredding the muscle, nicking an artery, shattering the bone—and the only thing that had helped was the stray dog that had attached itself to him on his way to the car after therapy one day.

A scraggly big-eared mutt Lex had named Honey because of her golden color. She'd been dirty and half-starved and she'd looked at him with the most haunted and hopeless big brown eyes and he hadn't thought twice about taking her home. She'd spent the first night on the rug next to his bed and, following a particularly horrible nightmare, had moved into the bed, against his back. Within a week, the dreams had stopped and there was something about her reassuring presence—knowing that they'd sort of saved each other—that made him feel like he was on his way to a recovery of sorts.

He'd always been an animal lover and inevitably ended up caring for the various strays on whatever base he was living. Having the dog to talk to, when he didn't want to talk to anyone else, having the dog to take for walks and care for, had helped him in ways that he wasn't even sure he could put into words. She'd loved him—unconditionally and quietly—and the difference she'd made in his world was phenomenal.

Thankfully Payne had assured him that the apartment that came with his unbelievably generous employment package was pet-friendly, and he also hadn't had any objections to Lex taking Honey along with him on this first assignment. Naturally Lex knew there were going to be times when he'd need to find someone to keep her for him and, as an added bonus, Payne had mentioned that his wife was a vet and would be happy to board the dog when the need arose.

Overall, despite the guilt and the injury—his shoulder wasn't ever going to be right again—Lex felt like he was closer to being where he should be than he'd been in a very long time. And rather than doing what was expected or what he knew would meet with approval, he was going to find his ultimate purpose and pursue it with as much energy as he could. Did that mean he intended this to be a transition job, that he'd hired on with the intent of leaving? No. But he was never again going to be so wedded to a career that he couldn't make the most of his life.

As a result of almost dying on the battlefield, he had a whole new appreciation for life, and wanted to live it to the fullest. Every choice, every decision—from what he had for breakfast to what he was going to do with the rest of his life—held infinitely more significance.

Almost dying would do that to you. Among other things…

"You're all settled into your apartment?" Payne asked.

"Yes." It was very nice and, lucky for him, fully furnished. The place had been outfitted with every possible convenience. Much like the "boardroom" they were currently in, it had state-of-the-art appliances and electronics and had been decorated with an eclectic mix of old and new. The old had more than likely come from Bess Cantrell, he realized now. The cabinets and fridge had been stocked with essentials and a bottle of Jameson—a gift from Jamie—had been on his counter.

The apartment had previously belonged to Seth McCutcheon, who had recently married and moved into his new bride's house in Marietta. Evidently he made the drive into Atlanta when necessary, but otherwise, mostly worked from home. Lex hadn't met him yet, but everyone else spoke highly of him.

Despite the fact that he'd lived in different places all over the world, Lex had to admit that the South would always be home. Originally he was from Blue Creek, Alabama—a sweet little town that sat right on the banks of the Tennessee River—but Atlanta was a mere four-hour drive. He hadn't been this close to home since he'd graduated high school, and while he didn't have any desire to move back—they practically rolled up the streets at five o'clock—he did like the fact that he could make a quick run over for Sunday dinner and that he would be close enough to visit his parents, and his sister and her children, for holidays and the occasional barbecue.

All the things he'd missed, Lex thought with an inward sigh.

"Are you satisfied with the employment package?" Jamie asked.

Lex smiled. "Quite."

"You'll earn it," Guy told him. "We offer an extremely specialized service and, as such, our clients pay accordingly. Without our former Rangers—some of the best-trained soldiers in the world, as you know—we couldn't offer a fraction of the expertise that we do."

In other words they needed him and were only paying him what they thought he was worth. He just hoped he didn't disappoint them. Before he'd been shot he wouldn't have had a problem accepting such an amount, but now…

"If we didn't think you were able to do this job, we wouldn't have hired you," Payne said, his cool blue eyes missing nothing. "We've reviewed your discharge papers, looked at the medical report. We're confident that you're going to be able to meet the physical requirements of the job."

Lex released a small breath and nodded. "If I ever reach a point where I can't, then you can rest assured that I'll tell you. I'd never compromise an assignment for my pride." He grinned and shot them a look. "Much as I might want to," he added.

McCann laughed and the other two chuckled. "I think it's safe to say that's something we could all identify with."

Lex released a pent-up breath. "So when do I get started?"

"Now," Payne told him. He handed him the file. "The address is on the front. You've got a GPS, right?"

He nodded.

"Good," Payne continued. "Bess has her client list, you've got your laptop and it interfaces with all the technology here at the office. If you need us for anything, then don't hesitate to call."

Payne stood, prompting everyone else to get to

their feet, and extended his hand. "Welcome aboard," he said.

"Thanks," Lex told him. "It's good to be here."

And it was. Or it would be, provided he could prove himself with this first assignment.

PAYNE WATCHED LEX SANBORN close the door behind him and waited until he was certain he was out of earshot. He turned to Jamie and Guy and arched a brow. "Well?"

"Much as Garrett has been a pain in the ass, I actually think we need to do something for the old bastard," Guy remarked, settling back into the recliner. "He sure as hell knows what he's doing when it comes to sending us recruits."

"I think Lex is still a little unsure of that shoulder," Jamie said, "but otherwise he seems like he's got it together."

Payne agreed. In fact, he actually thought that Lex was going to transition better than a lot of their other agents. Because he'd been through it himself, he could tell that Lex felt guilty for coming out of the service during a time of war and that was completely natural. He'd been career military until a week ago, and leaving friends behind—particularly ones in the line of fire—was never easy.

But Payne was also pulling another vibe from Lex, one that he couldn't exactly put his finger on, but if he had to label it… Relief maybe? He'd been hit, had almost died. That would certainly be understandable.

Jamie chuckled. "Is he really going to take that dog with him?"

Payne nodded and smiled. He considered himself an animal lover and was married to a vet, so he completely understood being devoted to one's animals, but even he had to admit he'd never seen anything quite like Lex and Honey. The dog was never more than a foot or two away from Lex and stayed in front of him, as though always ready to put herself between any potential threat and her master. And that adoration was clearly returned.

"Bess won't mind," Payne said. "And like he said, leaving her alone when they've only been in the building a few days would be hard on the dog."

"Even with Emma watching her?" Guy asked. "She's like Mother Teresa to the entire animal kingdom."

Payne chuckled. "I'll be sure to tell her you said that."

Jamie nodded thoughtfully. "I think he's going to be a good addition to the team."

Payne did, too.

Guy grinned. "Do you think we should have mentioned that Bess isn't—"

"Nah," Jamie told him, a big grin spreading across his face. "He'll find out soon enough."

Payne smiled. He most certainly would.

2

BESS CANTRELL OBSERVED the mutinous look on her assistant's face and heaved an internal sigh of frustration. In addition to everything else that was going wrong, she did not need Elsie's drama. But if she hadn't wanted drama, she should have never kept on the spotty psychic/occasional nudist/full-time pain in the ass as her help after her grandfather died.

"I've got a bad feeling about this," Elsie predicted. "You never listen to me, but you're going to wish you did this time. I know I'm not always spot-on—"

Bess gave a mental eye roll. "You mean like the time you told me that you saw me taking a beach vacation and the pipes burst beneath the kitchen sink?"

"—but I'm telling you, *this* time—"

Bess tidied her client list once again, then slipped it into a folder. "Or the time you told me that you saw me having a hot night of passion with the UPS man and the next day his face was on the front page of the paper for setting a warehouse ablaze?"

Elsie's papery cheeks flushed, but she continued on. "Be that as it may, I have a terrible, terrible feeling that you're going to get—"

Bess heaved a deep sigh. "Or the time you told me that I shouldn't go to the grocery store on Lentil, to go to one on Hillengrove because you were certain that the one on Lentil was going to have some sort of trouble, and I went to Hillengrove and was held hostage for over an hour while the store was being burgled?"

"I got those two confused!" Elsie finally exploded, her dark penciled eyebrows winging up her forehead. "My sight isn't perfect! How many times do I have to explain that to you? But the point is I was right about something terrible happening." She grimaced primly. "I merely got the store wrong," she said, as if this little detail didn't signify.

And in Elsie's mind, it didn't.

Bess looked out the storefront and continued to wait for the agent Brian Payne, one of her good clients, was sending over. She didn't have any idea how much his services actually cost—and would have been more than willing to pay—but Brian had insisted on trading the service out. As such, she was going to be on the lookout for anything she thought he might be interested in. Over the years he'd bought everything from old lighting fixtures to antique clear gas pumps. He had eclectic taste and had been a good customer.

When the police had failed to give her any true hope of catching the person who'd stolen her hard drive and was now in the process of harassing her clients, Brian had been the first person she'd thought of. She'd had no idea that the book in the picture had actually been a Wicked Bible and, furthermore, had had no idea that a thing like that even existed. But given that Brian had told her he knew of one that had gone for a hundred grand at auction recently, she could certainly understand the appeal.

Elsie released a self-suffering sigh. "You aren't going to listen to me, are you?" she said, frowning tragically. "I have this sight—this gift," she continued with a theatrical wave toward the sky. "And you are going to go about your mulish, headstrong ways." She harrumphed. "You are *just* like your grandfather. Always have been, even when you were just a wee thing."

"Thank you," Bess said, even though she knew Elsie didn't exactly mean it as a compliment. She'd loved her grandfather to utter distraction and had appreciated everything about him. She'd lost him three years ago and there wasn't a day that went by when she didn't miss him terribly. Her father had died in a car wreck when she was seven and her mother, racked with grief, had taken her own life a year later on the anniversary of his death. Officially orphaned then, she'd moved in with her grandfather—a widower himself—and had been with him ever since. So had Elsie, for that matter, which was no small reason why Bess didn't let her go and hire someone more competent. But Elsie tried and, though there had never been anything romantic between the older woman and her grandfather, she'd been the closest thing to a grandmother Bess had ever had. Since she'd always collected odd things, Elsie fit in perfectly.

Her grandfather's house was hers now, of course, and Bess had renovated it more to her liking, but there were certain things she hadn't been able to touch. His tobacco stand still sat next to his old leather tufted wingback chair and the small needlepoint footstool was still stationed in front of it, waiting for a pair of aching feet. She grinned.

Usually hers.

They'd made quite a pair, she and her grandfather. Though he hadn't told her until much, much later, she hadn't spoken at all for the first year after her mother had committed suicide. She'd nod or shake her head and occasionally cry, but she hadn't talked and she hadn't smiled. Rather than send her back to school before she was ready, he'd homeschooled her instead and, though he'd tried to reintroduce her to public school later, she'd become so distraught he'd refused to make her go.

Beyond second grade she hadn't set foot in a classroom until she'd gone to college, and even then she would have rather been tutored by her grandfather. Frankly, her education would have been better. She'd learned the Classics at his knee, could read bits of Latin and knew more about the solar system than the general population. He'd taught her Roman and Greek mythology, had taken her to almost every major battlefield in the continental U.S. and had made history so alive for her, it was a passion she still had today.

They'd ride the back roads of the South "picking," as he liked to call it, and he'd drill her on various mathematical theorems and throw out famous quotes and expect her to know them, based on all the biographies he'd wanted her to read. "I cannot live in a world without books" had been one of his favorites. Thomas Jefferson, she remembered.

Her grandfather had wanted her to have the degree in the event she ever decided to do anything besides "rescue history," picking through old barns and houses for people's "junk," though she *abhorred* that term. Nothing was *ever* junk in her opinion. Everything had value and purpose.

To the illiterate eye her place was probably a catchall for useless items, but to Bess it was a cache of things that had almost been lost. She was holding on to them for safekeeping until they could be sold and passed on to someone who would appreciate them.

"I can see you've made your mind up," Elsie continued, her nostrils flaring.

The luggage next to the door had probably "told" her that, Bess thought, squashing a smile.

"I have. Brian is sending someone over to keep watch on the store so you'll be safe, and I'll have my cell if anything comes up while I'm off with the additional agent." She sent her a harsh look. "And by 'comes up' I mean a legitimate issue, not any premonitions, you understand."

Elsie tsked and shook her head. "Poor Nostradamus," she said. "I have an inkling right now how he must have felt."

Bess smothered a snort. "Just cover the store and handle the auctions, please. Hopefully we'll be able to take care of this relatively quickly."

Where was the agent anyway? The longer it took them to get on the road, the more time the asshole who was terrorizing her clients had to get ahead of them. One of the advantages she and the agent would have was that Bess knew which clients were ones she'd sold stuff to and which clients she'd bought things from. The would-be thief was drawing from a master list and had been going to see both, and he was working in a pretty direct line, moving from place to place. If he kept to this pattern, then they should be able to catch up with him.

Initially Brian had tried to talk her out of going along, as well, but he soon gave that thought up. These were her clients, with whom she had credibility, and it was her foolish mistake that had put them all in jeopardy.

To be fair, it was her practice to take pictures on-site, particularly if the piece was going to be something she'd put up for auction online. It was faster to do it that way and it made the process a whole lot simpler. She'd come in from the road, upload the photos, write the descriptions and activate the auction. If things needed a bit more cleaning up before selling, she'd do that once she got back to the store, but for the most part, her clientele didn't care if something was "clean." Like her, they could look at it and see the potential. Furthermore, collectors weren't as picky.

If only she could remember where she'd gotten that Coca-Cola sign, Bess thought for what had to have been the millionth time. She'd racked her brain, had gone through everything she'd had on auction during that time, and could not recall where she'd gotten the sign. It could have been someone she regularly visited or someone she'd never picked before. If she saw promise—barns, old buildings, rusty cars and bicycles in the yard—she'd stop and do a cold call. She always kept a record of what she bought, but the truth was she'd bought *dozens* of Coca-Cola signs—the brand was highly collectible—and it could have come from any one of those places.

Luckily she'd been in the process of trying to organize those records and had off-loaded them onto her laptop, so the—she was just going to call him Bastard—didn't have access to them.

And really, without those particular records, Bastard was looking for a needle in a haystack. She took a mild amount of satisfaction from that.

"Ooo, I think he's here," Elsie murmured, peering out the window. She patted her extremely teased hair and moistened her heavily painted lips. "That has to be him. Nice khakis, black cable-knit sweater—you know how I love a cable-knit sweater on a man." She gasped. "And, oh, look! He's brought a dog!"

He had, Bess thought, watching covertly off to one side of Elsie, who was positioned behind the counter. While she would have ordinarily been more interested in the animal than the man, it was the man that held her attention right now.

Mercy.

Bess sucked in a shallow breath as every hair on her body suddenly prickled with goose bumps. Her heart galloped into overdrive and her mouth instantly parched, forcing her to swallow. She felt a bizarre sort of tug behind her navel and then a swirl of heat slid into her belly and settled there, making her more aware of the warmth than was strictly comfortable.

He was big and broad-shouldered with dark brown hair that was more swept to the side than styled, and the way that it clung to his head made her want to slide her hands through it, to see if it was as sleek as it looked. He had a face that was incredibly masculine—broad planes and angles, a nose that had been broken at least once—but an especially full mouth that gave him a slightly boyish quality, one she instinctively imagined he resented.

But the mouth was…incredible. She licked her own lips as she stared at his and wondered what it would be like to kiss him, to feel his lips against hers. Her nipples beaded behind her bra and she released a small sigh and leaned closer to the window.

As Elsie had pointed out, he wore khakis that showcased long legs, a narrow waist and, from the side anyway, an ass that was nice and tight. The sweater stretched over a pair of heavily muscled shoulders, clung to an equally muscled chest and basically let a woman know that there was a rock-hard, beautifully maintained body beneath the clothes. The only part of him that she couldn't truly see were his eyes, which were hidden behind a pair of designer aviator sunglasses she desperately wished weren't in the way. *I bet he has brown eyes,* Bess thought, imagining a warm dark chocolate with long sooty lashes.

He opened the car door and clipped a leash to the dog, a blond mutt of questionable origins, but pretty all the same, and the animal leaped down onto the pavement. He scoped both ends of the sidewalk before studying the storefront and she watched his lips—that sinfully carnal mouth—twist with something akin to humor, but not as kind. A pinprick of disappointment nicked her heart, but she shrugged it off. Just because he was the most gorgeous man she'd ever seen in her life didn't mean he was going to be any different from the rest.

Sad, that, she thought, because her reaction to him had certainly been different from previous reactions to any man she'd ever seen in print, in person or in film.

She got the impression that he'd taken one look at her business, gotten her measure and had already— even though he hadn't met her yet—found her lacking.

The bell over the door tinkled as he walked in and he went immediately to the counter, stuck out his hand and introduced himself. He'd removed the sunglasses along the way, but to her irritation, she couldn't get a good look at his eyes. "Lex Sanborn, Ms. Cantrell," he said. "It's a pleasure to meet you."

Elsie, who was hardly what one would call a wallflower, smiled brightly at him. "It's a pleasure to meet you, too," she said, lowering her voice to a husky purr à la Lana Turner.

Bess smothered a snort and then had to cover her hand with her mouth when she caught Lex's temporarily transfixed expression. Evidently he was picturing going on the road with a lusty senior citizen intent on making him her boy toy. After the look he'd given her shop, he could just keep that image, Bess thought, and stayed out of view.

He tried to withdraw his hand, but Elsie clung firm. She had closed her eyes, evidently going into one of her psychic trances. She murmured a nonsensical noise and gave a delicate shudder. "You came very close, didn't you?" she said.

Lex gave an uneasy laugh. "I'm sorry?"

Elsie patted the top of his hand and, when she opened her eyes, her expression was strangely warm and sad. "But it wasn't your time."

Some of the color leached from his face and the dog nuzzled his leg as though picking up on a shift in its master's mood. "Er…if you're ready, we should probably get going."

Bess frowned, puzzled over his reaction, and shot a look at Elsie, who seemed to have wilted against the stool behind the counter. The older woman very rarely looked her age—on purpose—but at the moment she seemed every one of her seventy-five years. What had happened? Bess wondered.

Elsie finally seemed to snap out of whatever had a hold of her. "Go? Go where?"

Lex smiled uncertainly. "After the man who has stolen your hard drive and is harassing your customers," he reminded her, and it was obvious he thought she was a touch senile.

Elsie chuckled. "Oh, I'm not going," she told him, as if he were the one who was confused.

He blinked. "You're not?"

"No, Bess is," she explained.

He gave his head a shake. "You're not Bess?"

Elsie positively cackled with laughter. "Goodness, no," she said. "But I wouldn't mind being her for a few days," she confided with a wink and, though Elsie's comment was wasted on Lex, Bess knew it was in reference to her youth. Elsie often accused her of "squandering" it with old junk, cable internet and reality television, which was hardly fair when she'd caught Elsie watching *Real Housewives,* as well.

Elsie looked past Lex's shoulder and he instinctively turned around.

"I'm Bess," she said, coming forward. His gaze slammed into hers and, though she knew it was impossible, she practically floated the rest of the way across the room, tugged inexplicably by the pull of his stare. She felt a smile drift over her lips and released a slow steady breath.

Mystery solved, she thought.

His eyes were blue. And she was drowning.

3

HE COULDN'T HAVE BEEN more stunned if he'd been knocked over the head with a frying pan, Lex thought as he watched the woman come toward him.

In the first place, she was young. As in *not* old. Or not as old as he'd assumed she would be, at any rate. He struggled to get a handle on this change of events. Just a second ago he'd been certain he'd walked into his worst nightmare, a geriatric cougar bent on hunting him the entire trip.

In the second place, she was beautiful. Not mildly attractive or merely pretty.

Bess Cantrell was beautiful.

She had long wavy auburn hair and big green eyes that tilted upward at the corners, giving her an exotic edge. Curly lashes framed those compelling eyes, especially high cheekbones carved lovely hollows beneath them, and her nose was small and finely made.

She had the clearest, smoothest skin he'd ever seen, and though he'd never understood the phrase "porcelain complexion," he did now. The mouth that tied this all together was lush and bow-shaped and curled just so on the upper lip to make one think she was enjoying a bit of a private joke. At your expense.

She was petite and very curvy, probably carrying more weight than was currently fashionable, but he'd never liked a scrawny girl. He'd always imagined sex with a so-called supermodel would be like bedding a praying mantis. Sorry, not for him. He preferred the soft womanly frame of the old Hollywood stars—the pinup girls circa WWII—and this girl would have been right at home on the nose of a B-52.

The private joke he'd caught between his employers now made perfect sense and he felt his own lips twist with belated humor. A warning would have been nice, but wouldn't have been nearly as enjoyable for them. Sneaky bastards. Perversely, he liked them even more now than he did before.

Bess shook his hand, the small touch resonating to the soles of his feet, then leaned forward and spoke in conspiratorial undertones. "I hope I'm the lesser of two evils," she said with a tiny significant jerk of her head toward the woman behind the counter. Her voice was light and musical with a husky finish that put him in mind of tangled sheets and naked skin.

Hers specifically.

Lex smiled. He wasn't touching that loaded remark with a ten-foot pole. "Lex Sanborn," he said. "With Ranger Security."

She nodded. "Bess Cantrell. It's a pleasure to meet you." Her gaze dropped down to his dog and her naturally pink tinted lips slid into a friendly grin. "And who is this?"

"Honey," he said. "I hope you don't mind that I've brought her along."

"Not at all," she said. "She's a pretty dog." She dropped down to face Honey and held her hand out so that the animal could get a sniff. Honey looked up at him, evidently seeking approval, and, at his nod, she nosed Bess's palm. The ice broken, Bess petted her head and scratched her behind the ears. "Ahhh," she said, grinning at the animal. "You like that, do you? You're a good girl." She was completely at ease talking to the dog. Some people weren't, which he thought was odd. He'd always found it easier to get along with animals than people, a fact he'd forgotten until he'd found Honey.

Bess stood again and looked up at him. "So we'd better be going then?"

He nodded, annoyed that she'd had to remind him and not the other way around. What the hell was wrong with him? It's not like he'd never seen a beautiful woman. Not like he hadn't been with more than a few actually. So what was it about *this* one that had made him forget himself already? What was it about this one that had his balls tightening and his chest in knots? After less than *thirty seconds* in her company?

Bess went over and hugged the woman behind the counter. "I'll check in often, Elsie, and call me if something important comes up." She lingered purposely over the "important" part, leading him to believe that the bizarre Elsie was prone to contacting her about things that weren't. Given what he'd observed in the minute he'd known Elsie, he could see where that would definitely have been the case. When she'd refused to release his hand and made the you've-come-close remark, he'd gotten the strangest sensation that the older woman had been peering directly into his brain, picking his secrets out, leaving him more than a little unnerved.

His gaze slid to Bess once more and lingered over her ripe rear end. Most definitely the lesser of two evils, he thought.

"Of course," Elsie said with an innocent bat of her lashes.

"And you'll feed Severus for mc?"

"Every morning and afternoon to make sure that his blood sugar stays normal." She snorted. "And cats are supposed to be low-maintenance pets."

Bess smiled gratefully at the older woman. "Thanks, Elsie. You're a peach." She turned to face him once again and then headed toward the door and picked up an overnight bag. "I'm ready when you are."

He hurried forward and took the bag from her hand, then opened the door for her, making the effort to remember that he *was* a gentleman and had been taught common courtesies.

"I could have gotten that," she said. "Believe me, I'm used to carrying things a lot heavier."

He imagined so. Nevertheless, he'd do the heavy lifting on this trip. He opened the car door for her and tried not to watch the way the denim clung to her luscious heart-shaped ass as she slipped into the passenger seat. Muttering a plea for self-restraint, he stored her bag in the back of the SUV next to his, then helped Honey into the backseat and unclipped her leash.

"She's going to hate me for riding shotgun, isn't she?" Bess remarked, glancing back at his dog. He loved the way her hair curved along her sleek jaw, over her shoulders and around one breast. It was sexy and sensual and utterly effortless on her part, which naturally made it all the more appealing. His dick stirred behind his zipper, forcing him to shift into a more comfortable position.

This was *so* not good, Lex thought as he slid the key into the ignition and started the car. He looked over his shoulder and then pulled out into traffic, belatedly realizing that he had no idea where they were going. In retrospect, he should have gone over that with her *before* leaving the store.

Too late now.

Not off to a very auspicious start, Lex thought, feeling more and more out of control.

"She'll be fine," he said, finally answering her question about the dog. "Payne brought me up to speed on what is going on and mentioned that your thief has been moving from one address to the next closest. Is this correct?" There, he thought. That sounded semiprofessional.

"It is," she confirmed. She pulled a paper from a folder she'd had in her bag and consulted it for a moment. "Based on the address of the last incident he should be going down toward Waycross."

"Waycross?"

"Yes, if he's continuing to the next closest address. I figure he'll stay within Georgia before going toward Mississippi, Tennessee or the Carolinas."

He felt his eyes widen. Good grief, he'd had no idea they could potentially be covering that kind of ground, much less that in her quest for junk *she* covered that kind of ground. Had Payne left that little tidbit out of the briefing? Lex wondered, or had he just missed it?

"Have you alerted your clients in Waycross?" he asked, trying to quickly pull together a plan.

"Client," she corrected. "And yes I have. Gus has been put on alert, knows that I haven't sent anyone as my representative and he doesn't have anything remotely resembling the book. He's armed, and if anyone comes up on his property and doesn't heed him, they're liable to get the shock of their lives."

"Sounds like this guy needs it," Lex remarked with a grunt. "Have you had breakfast?"

She blinked, seemingly confused by the sudden subject change. "Breakfast?"

"First meal of the day," he said. "From the late Middle English *breakfast,* meaning to break one's fast."

"I know what it is," she said, shooting him an exasperated smile. "But thanks for the etymology lesson all the same."

He couldn't help it. It wasn't enough to know what a word meant, he wanted to know where it had come from, as well. He was an avid crossword fan and he found that knowing a word's origin often helped him figure things out. He'd picked the habit up from his grandfather, who'd also been in the service, and had been working them ever since.

"Well?" he pressed.

She looked confused again, as though they weren't having the same conversation. "Well what?"

He chuckled. "Have you had breakfast?"

She grinned. "I have, actually, but if you haven't, then I certainly don't mind watching you eat."

"I've already eaten, too," he told her. "But I think we need to plot our route a little more thoroughly, so why don't we stop for a quick cup of coffee and work that out?"

She nodded. "Sure. That sounds good."

He found a coffeehouse with an outside eating area for Honey, and Bess stayed with the dog while he went in and ordered for them. The air had a bit of a chill to it, but thankfully not so cold as to be unpleasant. Bess had tied Honey's leash to a chair and was busy petting the dog, who naturally had her head angled toward the store until he came out.

"She doesn't like it when she can't see you," Bess remarked when he returned with their drinks and a Danish apiece. He handed Bess her spiced apple cider and took a chair opposite her. Honey immediately came to sit at his feet, resting her chin against his knee. He patted her head and rubbed her velvety ears. "She's awfully devoted. How long have you had her?"

"About five months," Lex told her.

She took a sip of her drink and he noticed she'd donned a kelly green hat, a matching scarf and fingerless gloves. Impossibly, she looked even more gorgeous. "So she wasn't a puppy when you got her?"

"No. According to the vet she's about a year and

a half." He tore off a piece of apple tart and put it in his mouth. "What about you? What's a Severus?" he asked, remembering her instructions to Elsie.

She laughed softly. "A Severus is a black cat and he's the unofficial boss of my house."

"Unofficial boss?"

"I'm the official one," she confided. "I just don't tell him that."

"And this is Severus, as in Severus Snape, the much-vilified and hated Potions Master at Hogwarts School of Witchcraft and Wizardry?"

She gasped delightedly. "A hobby etymologist *and* you know your Harry Potter."

He'd read the books while he'd been recovering. It was the first time in years that he'd had so much time to simply be still, and he'd heard the books were filled with a lot of literary references and mythology. He'd enjoyed every minute of them.

"They were incredible," he said. But nice as this was, it wasn't getting them any closer to their goal. He snagged the maps on the table and picked up a red ink pen. "In order to make sure we know exactly where we're going and where we are in relation to where he might be, I think we need to mark everything off on the map and then go from there."

She pulled an atlas from her bag and opened it to Georgia. "You mean like this?" she asked.

Lex was genuinely beginning to wonder exactly

why he was here. "Yes, like that exactly," he said, shooting her a forced smile.

Evidently catching the slight snarl behind his grin, she chuckled. "I'm sorry," she said, her green eyes twinkling with humor. "I did this last night. As I understood it, they were only bringing you up to speed this morning and I thought it might be helpful."

It was helpful and he had no reason to be irritated or feel like she'd lopped his balls off and handed them to him, but he did. This was his first assignment and so far she'd done all the work. It was time for him to start earning his money.

"It is helpful," he said. He snagged the book and flipped through it. She'd marked up all the surrounding states, as well, everywhere she'd been. It was very thorough, very meticulous and he couldn't have done a better job himself. Still, he hadn't done it, and that was the problem.

He looked up at her and released a pent-up breath. "Let me ask you something, Bess."

"Sure."

"Are you a good shot?"

She frowned, seemingly confused. "You mean with a gun?"

"Yes."

She sucked in a breath, released it and shrugged. "Not particularly," she demurred.

Good, he thought. Then maybe he'd be of some

actual use on this assignment. Provided he got to shoot at someone. Preferably not himself, though intuition told him he was going to need some form of distraction to put him out of his misery—that of the sexual variety—before this was over.

SHE HADN'T REALLY LIED, Bess thought. She wasn't a good shot—she was an *excellent* shot. Good implied mediocre, and she was far from just good. After her mother had committed suicide, Bess had been utterly terrified of guns. She'd go into a fit of terror if a car backfired, if she heard a fake gunshot on television. Simply seeing one sent her into a panic.

Given the way she'd reacted, one would have thought that she'd been in the house when her mother had taken her own life, but that wasn't the case. Her mother, bereaved and out of her right mind as she was, had at least had the forethought and kindness to send Bess over to a friend's to play. She'd attached a note to the front door to prevent anyone from letting her child into the house so that Bess wouldn't be the one to find her. A second note for Bess, with a simple "I'm sorry" at the end of it for her, was tucked behind a picture of the three of them together, Bess and her mom and dad, one of the few she had from her childhood.

At any rate, convinced that the only thing that was going to get her over her fear of guns was learning to handle one herself, her grandfather had taken her out for target practice over and over again and proved to be delighted when she'd been a natural. Regardless of what kind of piece he put in her hand, be it a pistol or a rifle, she always came within an inch of the bull's eye.

Her gaze slid to Lex, who was going over the maps, evidently plotting their route. Somehow she didn't think it was a good idea to tell him that she was an excellent marksman. He was already feeling relatively useless, if she had her guess.

But just because she could plot a map and fire a gun didn't mean she'd actually have the guts to shoot someone if it came down to it. She'd like to think that she could do it to defend her own life or someone else's, but she'd never been in that situation.

As a former Ranger she knew he had, and she also knew that she couldn't be in better hands.

But she didn't need to think about being in his hands, because that ignited a thought process that took her imagination to depraved places it had no business going and made her panties feel like they'd been dipped in steam.

His eyes weren't just blue, as she'd noted before. They were a bizarre mix of blue and green with a darker ring of lapis around the edges. They were utterly arresting, the shade managing to be both bright and dark, like the sky in a Maxfield Parrish painting, so perfect it had earned the name "Parrish Blue."

She'd known the minute she'd looked at him that she was going to be in trouble, that she was going to want him with an intensity far beyond anything in her experience. On a physical level, he simply did it for her. He was big and hard and exuded confidence without being cocky, and there was an irreverence in his gaze, in the shape of that droll, incredibly carnal mouth, that was particularly attractive.

Something about the line of his jaw against his neck when he turned his head just so made her long to slip her fingers along that bone, to trace the shell of his ear. Everything about him was masculine and beautiful, even the way his hair lay against his scalp. She watched his fingers trace a path along the map and her belly gave a clench. His hands were large and veined and the strength in them was palpable. She imagined them kneading her flesh and released a sigh deep enough to draw his attention.

She felt a blush race to her hairline and took another sip of her cider.

"Is something wrong?" he asked.

Only with her misguided libido, Bess thought. She blinked innocently. "No."

His lips twitched with humor.

"Are you laughing at me?" she asked, waiting to

watch the way his mouth moved when he talked. It was sensual and mesmerizing.

"No," he said. "Not at you."

"But something was funny?"

He dropped the pen in his hand and leaned back and regarded her more thoroughly. That lazy scrutiny made her stomach flutter and warm. "Yes, actually. I was thinking you must have learned that little innocent look you just gave me from Elsie because it was the same exact blinking incomprehension that she gave you when you told her not to call unless it was important."

She popped a bite of Danish into her mouth and laughed. "It's possible that I picked it up from her," she said. "I've known her most of my life."

"She's quite a character," he said, which she thought was more charitable than saying she was crazy as a shit-house rat, which was what most everyone else thought about her. Including Bess, if she were honest, but it only added to Elsie's charm.

"She is," Bess said with a nod. "She has the sight, you know."

"The what?"

"She likes to think she's psychic," Bess clarified, and wondered again what had spooked him so much when Elsie had taken his hand. Something had, she was sure. And for all his irreverent nonchalance, there was an unexplained shadow in his gaze—

almost haunted-looking—that made her wonder about his story. Everyone, in her experience, had a story and she found herself unbelievably intrigued by his.

It was his turn to blink and she chuckled again. "Seems like you're a quick study on the look, as well," she told him, wrapping her hands around her drink to keep them warm.

A rustle of leaves swept along the sidewalk and pots of mums bloomed in burgundy and yellow batches around the little patio. She loved fall, Bess thought. It was her favorite season, when the harvest peaked and Mother Nature, proud of her accomplishment, settled in and took a much-needed rest. Every wind felt like her sigh, and Bess huddled more snugly into her jacket.

"She rattled you, didn't she?" Bess prodded, knowing he more than likely wouldn't answer, but curious all the same.

He bit the inside of his cheek. "You mean when she practically slithered across the counter toward me and lowered her voice into that alarmingly breathy purr?"

She felt her own lips twitch. "Elsie likes younger men."

He grinned and quirked a brow. "Do they typically like her?"

She chuckled again, unable to help herself. "She's managed to date a few younger men."

"And by younger, you still mean they are senior citizens?"

"Yes," she said, snickering.

"Aha," he said. "I thought so. I'm less than half her age." He gave a shudder. "I almost feel like I need a bath."

Laughing quietly, Bess felt her eyes water. "Oh, come on," she said. "It can't have been as bad as that."

"It was," he deadpanned. "Because I thought she was you."

Her sides were aching. "Yes, I know," she wheezed.

His eyes widened in outrage. "You know? You knew?" He gasped. "You were watching," he accused. "You saw the whole damned thing, didn't you?"

She nodded, unable to respond.

"That's... That's...*evil,*" he said, staring at her with a new sort of appreciation in his eyes.

She merely shrugged. "I saw you when you got out of the car," she said. "I might have corrected you, but you were in such a hurry and then—" she pressed her lips together to keep from grinning again "—and then it was just too funny not to watch."

He shook his head, continued to stare at her, then sketched a makeshift bow. "Glad to provide your entertainment, milady. Let me know when I can do it again."

Ooo-la-la, Bess thought as the last words rolled off that incredibly smooth tongue. She had a feeling he could provide her with hours and hours of hot, sweaty, wonderfully wicked entertainment if she'd let him.

And judging by the heat scorching her veins, she just might before this trip was through.

4

AFTER AN HOUR IN BESS'S company, Lex was beginning to wonder if he might have been better off protecting his virtue from Elsie than essentially being trapped in the car with a woman he'd wanted to lick from head to toe the first moment he'd set eyes on her.

Licking, he was relatively sure, wasn't in his job description, and considering that he was already feeling like he wasn't doing the damned thing properly—that she'd beaten him to a plan, as it were—he didn't need to further complicate matters by making a play for his…partner. He couldn't think of anything else to call her, really. She wasn't his client or his target or even his accomplice.

And more importantly, she was Brian Payne's friend. Brian had mentioned that he'd known Bess for years, that he'd been buying things from her for a long time and that her case was special. Though he hadn't said as much, Lex imagined that Bess was either trading him out inventory for services or she was getting a vastly reduced rate. He didn't have any idea what kind of money she pulled in through her store selling her ju—*stuff,* he mentally corrected, remembering Payne's warning about her dislike of the word, but he couldn't imagine that it was a huge income.

From the corner of his eye he watched her review her client list again, evidently trying to jog her memory into revealing where she'd bought the sign that would lead her to the book before the asshole could find it. Her brow wrinkled in concentration and she thoughtfully chewed a piece of gum, occasionally licking her lips in the process.

It was distracting as hell.

"Argh," she moaned, rubbing her temples. "You don't know how much I hate that I can't remember where I bought that sign. I keep a record of everything," she explained. "My grandfather was meticulous about it and wanted me to be the same. I know that it's here somewhere, that there's a clue to its whereabouts in this paperwork, but—"

"You inherited Bygone's from your grandfather?" he asked, liking the nostalgic name of her store.

She nodded, a soft smile curling her lips. "I did.

He started picking in his teens, opened the store and did it all the way up until he died."

"Picking?"

She sent him a self-conscious smile. "That's what we're called. People who 'pick' through other people's unwanted stuff, looking for rusty treasure and old gold."

"Sort of like Dumpster diving?"

"In a manner of speaking. But our Dumpsters are old barns and sheds, so-called junkyards, though that term sticks in my craw," she said, her eyes narrowing. "Nothing is *junk*. Everything has value. It's just waiting for the right person to find it."

He stilled as her logic sank in, then he grunted.

"What?" she asked, narrowing her gaze suspiciously.

"Nothing," he said, shooting her an evaluating look. "I'd just never thought of it that way."

She turned back to her list, but seemed pleased. "Most people don't. And history is getting carted off to the landfills faster than pickers can save it all." She paused. "That old man whose front yard is an overgrown graveyard for old cars, cast-iron tubs and bicycles? The county health departments are coming in and shutting him down, threatening to condemn his house or fine him if he doesn't clean it up."

"And you object?"

She was thoughtful for a moment. "I don't know,"

she said. "I can see where neighbors would complain, but then again it's *his* property, and so long as no one is getting hurt…" She shrugged. "I don't know. I just think it's a shame all the way around."

"So what are the kinds of things you like to rescue?" he asked, unbelievably intrigued with the way her mind worked. She wasn't just pretty, he decided. She was interesting, too.

Definitely a dangerous combination.

She grinned. "Everything," she said. "Advertising signs, old motorcycles and parts, cars, bicycles, streetlights and tin toys, cash registers, trunks and luggage." She shrugged again, looking wistful. "Anything, really."

"But surely you have special clients for particular things, right?"

"Oh, yeah," she said. "For instance, your boss is into restoring old cars and likes all the gas and oil stuff."

"He does?" Granted, he hadn't known Payne long enough to glean that kind of information, but he could see where it would fit. And he'd only want original parts if he was restoring something—because he was a perfectionist—and someone like Bess was exactly who he'd contact.

Her smile turned reminiscent. "I remember the first thing that I sold to him. A vintage hood ornament for a 1955 Oldsmobile Rocket 88."

He chuckled. "You can remember that but you can't remember where you got that Coca-Cola sign?" he teased.

She growled in frustration. "I know! It's driving me crazy! But you have to understand, I buy lots of Coca-Cola stuff because it's so collectible. And it never sits for long."

Lex had never had a collection—unless you counted the Playboy magazines he'd hidden beneath a loose floorboard in his room as a teen. But if he did, he'd collect something cool, like vintage Harley-Davidsons or something like that. He'd recently seen a man on television who was trying to sell his PEZ collection and, though Lex knew the iconic candy dispensers had been around a long time, he'd had no idea that people actually collected them.

He said as much to Bess. "I just don't get it. Why would anybody want that stuff?"

"Who knows?" she said. "His father might have started him on it, or a friend of a friend. People will collect anything that resonates with them. I've never understood the shot glass craze, but there it is. Go into any souvenir store anywhere in the world and you're going to find shot glasses."

That one he understood. They were small and inexpensive.

"What about the spoons and the thimbles?" he said. "Don't leave those out."

Another laugh bubbled up her throat. "I do have a few thimbles," she admitted. "But they're antiques and don't have Yosemite National Park across the front. They're also solid silver with pretty filigree."

"So you collect thimbles?" he asked.

"Among other things," she admitted, looking out the window. She propped her elbow against the door, then sighed and rested her head against her hand.

"That sounds intriguing."

She turned to look at him, her green eyes sparkling with humor. "It wasn't meant to be. I just have a little of everything. If it's pretty or I can find a place for it, I keep it."

He studied her again. "Does your house look like the inside of a Cracker Barrel?"

She chuckled. "Not quite," she said.

"Does your yard resemble Fred Sanford's?"

"Not at all," she said. "You saw my house. It was right across the street from the store."

He blinked, surprised. "The pickle-green house with the red door and white gingerbread?"

"That's not red," she said lifting her chin. "It's watermelon." She snorted and rolled her eyes. "Pickle green," she lamented. "All that work and you think my house looks like a pickle."

He chuckled. "I'm sorry," he said. "That's the only frame of reference I have for that particular color."

"It's called Gecko," she told him with an imperial arch of her brow.

He grunted. "In that case, I think pickle sounds better."

Another eye roll. "You would."

"It's in keeping with your food theme."

She looked at him. "Food theme?"

"You said the door was watermelon," he reminded her. "And gingerbread trim."

It was her turn to harrumph and she glanced over at him again, seemingly seeing him from a new perspective, as though he'd unwittingly handed her the secret to his brain. "You know, in a twisted sort of way that makes perfect sense."

He grinned at her and arched a brow. "Logic is twisted?"

"Yours is."

He gave his head a baffled shake. "Interestingly enough, I actually think you mean that as a compliment."

"I do," she said. "You're nothing like I thought you'd be."

Oh, man, there was no way in hell he was going to be able to let that go. "What do you mean?"

"I can't put my finger on it exactly," she said, pursing her ripe lips in brooding consideration.

He waited, and when she didn't respond, he prodded her again. "Would you try?"

"I don't know," she said, her gaze thoughtful. "I think I expected someone like Payne. Cool and autocratic, convinced that his way is the only way."

He hated to tell her this, but if she hadn't preempted him on everything, that's exactly the way he would have been.

"And I'm not?"

Her grin turned a bit wicked. "You would have been…if I'd let you."

And with that enigmatic comment, she said, "Oh, Rascal Flatts!" and turned the volume up on the stereo, effectively cutting him off before he could argue.

She'd been managing him all along, Lex realized with a flash of horrible insight. The manipulative, scheming wench. And she was right—he had let her.

But that was about to change.

SHE REALLY SHOULDN'T HAVE goaded him, Bess thought, but she hadn't been able to help herself. Yes, she'd needed to come along and yes, she liked being in charge. But she should have continued to maneuver him without him realizing it.

It would have been better.

Now she watched the light of battle flare in his eyes, his jaw imperceptibly harden, and knew she'd just waved a red flag in front of a very obstinate bull.

Sometimes she was a moron. And this was one of those times.

"Does your client in Waycross know to contact you if this guy shows up?" he asked, moving the conversation back into strictly professional territory.

"He does," she said.

"Does he know to try and get the man's name? To get his license plate number, if possible?"

"Er...no." She hadn't thought of that, Bess realized, no longer feeling quite so smug. But a peek from the corner of her eye told her that he was.

She pulled out her cell phone, looked up Gus's number and dialed. "Morning, Gus," she said when he answered. "This is Bess again. Any visitor yet?"

"He was just here," Gus told her. She gasped and looked significantly at Lex.

"He was just there? What happened?"

She felt Lex go on alert, watched him still and tune in to her end of the conversation.

"I did exactly what you told me to, Bess. I sent that rotten no-good scoundrel packing."

She felt nauseated. "Did he give you any problems?"

"Didn't have a chance to," he said, sounding quite pleased with himself. "He came walking up on foot because I'd closed the gate at the end of the drive and I fired a warning shot into the air."

Without waiting for him to confirm who he was? "Gus, are you sure it was him?"

"I'm sure. He said he was a friend of yours."

Ah. "Did he give you a name?"

"Seems like it, Bess, but I'll be hanged if I can remember what it is now. I was just so riled up, you know. Wasn't thinking about catching his name. I was more concerned with making him leave."

She peeked over at Lex again and bit her bottom lip. "Well, I sure am glad that you were ready for him, Gus, and I'm even sorrier that this was a problem for you at all."

"No worries, Bess. It's not your fault. The man broke into your store and stole from you. It's not like you sold my address to the wily bastard."

True, but she still felt responsible. She was going to have to rethink how she took photos for her auctions, that was for damned sure. "Listen, Gus, you didn't happen to notice what kind of car he was driving, did you?"

"Naw," he said. "My sight isn't as good as it used to be and my driveway is on the longish side, you understand."

"I do," she said. "No worries then."

"You still coming to see me?" Gus wanted to know.

They were a good three hours from Waycross and, if Bastard moved in the direction she thought he was going to, Valdosta was next on his list. She winced. "Better not, Gus. We need to keep moving and try to catch this guy."

"Let me know if I can do anything," the old man told her.

"I will. Thanks, Gus. You take care of yourself."

"I always do."

She disconnected and swore.

"He's been there and left?" Lex asked.

"Yes. Gus didn't catch a name or the make of the car, much less the license plate. He lives about a quarter of a mile off the road and has a gate at the end of his drive to discourage trespassers. Bastard parked there and walked in, despite the signs." She heaved a breath. "He's lucky Gus didn't shoot him. He was within his rights."

"Bastard?"

"That's what I've been calling him," she said, feeling suddenly hopeless. "In the absence of a name, that one fits pretty well, don't you think?"

He chuckled. "I've been calling him Asshole."

"Let's combine them," she suggested. "Asshole Bastard is pretty damned fitting."

Lex heaved a breath. "Asshole Bastard it is, then. So where is he going next?"

"Valdosta, I think," she said. "But I could be wrong. This is just assuming that he covers the southern points first, then circles around. Whether he'll head east or west remains to be seen and, unfortunately, we're not going to know until he turns up somewhere." Honestly, without a name or the make of a vehicle or any other sort of lead, they were at this guy's mercy.

"Then you'll need to alert your clients on each side."

She growled low in her throat. "This is just so damned frustrating. I've never had anything like this happen before."

"Have you ever inadvertently put a picture of a rare hundred-thousand-dollar item on your website before?" he asked.

"No," she said, knowing he was trying to make her feel better. In all truthfulness, she couldn't have anticipated this so there was no way she could have prevented it. Still… So many of her clients were elderly and lived alone. Burt Augustine had already gotten assaulted by this son of a bitch and had his place searched while he lay helpless on the floor. And whether it was logical or not, it felt like her fault.

"We're what? Three hours from Valdosta?"

"Give or take thirty minutes," she said.

"Call your client and let them know he could be on his way, then plug the address into the GPS and we'll head there, too."

"We're going to be too late again."

"Possibly," he admitted. "But we know where he

was and we'll keep going until we get close enough to catch him."

She sighed and shot him a look. "You sound so confident."

"That's because I am," he said, flashing her a smile. "Have a little faith."

"Because you're a former Ranger? Because you're one of the most highly trained soldiers on the planet? A bonafide badass?" she drawled.

He blinked and slid her a look, his decadent lips twitching with humor. "Yes," he said with a humble nod. "But I wasn't going to say it."

"Not to worry," she said. "Payne told me." She paused. "He said you'd come out of the military because of an injury." She was prying again, but she was curious. Too curious.

He didn't move a muscle, but she felt him flinch all the same. "I did." He waited a beat. "I got hit," he said, though it was clear he didn't want to tell her anything about it. "In the shoulder."

She winced and resisted the urge to touch him, to offer comfort. "I'm sorry."

"It's better than it was, but probably as good as it's going to get." He jerked his head toward the dog. "That's where I found Honey. She was sitting outside the rehab clinic, almost like she was waiting for me," he told her, laughing softly. "Sounds crazy, doesn't it?"

"Not at all," she said, looking at the dog with much more appreciation. She had a sneaking suspicion this animal had somehow known how much Lex had needed something to love, to take his mind off his injury. "And this job at Ranger Security is your first since you came out of the military?"

"It is," he said with a nod. "Which should give you even more comfort, because I can't afford to screw it up."

She chuckled and cocked her head. "Actually, I find that very reassuring."

"Good to know that my pressure to perform eases your mind," he drawled, a smile in his voice.

"Payne would probably fire you if you messed this up," she went on, needling him. "He's a friend of mine, you know."

He struggled to hide a smile. "I am aware of that, yes."

"So between screwing up and disappointing me, he'd be very displeased with you." She grinned at him, tsked low under her breath. "You're in a terrible position. You *have* to sort this out."

"I know," Lex said, his eyes crinkling at the corners. "Believe me, I am well aware of what's at stake here."

"He almost thinks of me like a little sister," she went on. "Like I'm family."

He slid her a sidelong glance. "You're enjoying this entirely too much, you know that?"

She merely smiled. "Hey, at this point I've got to take my pleasure where I can get it."

There was a pregnant silence in the car and she immediately regretted her choice of words. They had sexual connotation that she'd hadn't meant, but she could hardly say anything, otherwise she'd just be drawing even more attention to them.

Shit.

She felt his gaze drift over her legs, up her hip, along her side and over her breasts. She could practically feel that gaze like a caress, like a blue flame sliding over her. She felt it drift over her neck, her jaw and mouth and she absently licked her lips, getting warmer and more muddled by the second.

Her nipples tingled behind her bra and a deep throb built low in her belly, then drifted farther down until she had to gently press her legs together to relieve a bit of the pressure.

He saw her squirm, and a lazy smile so wicked she should have melted beneath it drifted over his beautiful mouth.

"We all have to take our pleasure where we can get it," he drawled, his voice pure sin.

And she knew he'd just gotten his.

5

LEX TOOK ADVANTAGE OF Bess's need for a bathroom break to pour Honey a bowl of water and then walk her over to a grassy area next to the convenience store to do her own necessary business.

"You're a good traveler," he told her, rubbing her between her ears when she was done. She'd made the drive over from Alabama with him and had been fine—he'd gone home to see his family before coming to Atlanta—so he'd been pretty confident that she wouldn't get carsick or whine. But it was nice to know that this was going to be an option, that when the assignment fit, he could take her with him.

Bess strolled toward them and gestured to the packet of beef jerky in her hand. "I got this for Honey," she said. "Is it all right if she has it?"

He grinned. "You will earn an eternal spot in her heart if you let her have that," he said.

Bess grinned and, smiling, opened the package, squatted down and offered the treat to Honey, who, smelling food, immediately walked forward and took it. She gulped the jerky down in one bite, then wagged her tail and looked expectantly at Bess.

Bess laughed. "I'll give you more later," she said, her warm gaze lingering on the animal. "Can't have your stomach getting upset."

"No," Lex agreed with a significant grimace. "That wouldn't be fun at all."

"You mean for you or her?"

"Both."

Another smile curled her lips and she reached into her jacket pocket and withdrew a package of peanuts and a bottle of Coke. "Here," she said, handing it to him. "I wasn't sure what sort of snack you liked, so I went with a Southern staple."

"Peanuts and Coke?" he asked, grinning. He hadn't had that in years, but could clearly remember his grandfather dumping salted peanuts into the old glass Coca-Cola bottles.

"Yep. Protein and sugar," she said. "A power combo."

Considering that they weren't going to have time to stop for lunch, he thought she'd made a wise choice. With any luck they'd close the bulk of the distance today and catch up to the guy tomorrow. Payne had alerted the proper authorities and they knew that one of his agents would be bringing the guy in so that he could answer for the theft at Bess's store. Needless to say, the authorities hadn't had a problem with the arrangement. Lex had everything he needed to transport their prisoner and was more than confident that he'd be able to handle him, whoever he turned out to be. The idea of enemy fire still made his heart race and a chill dread invade his limbs, but a bully? One who picked on the elderly? He actually looked forward to getting his hands on the guy.

They headed back to the car and got on the road again. Bess opened her own drink and then immediately started looking over another list, different from the one they were following. His curiosity piqued, he asked the obvious question.

"What's that you're looking at?"

"It's a list."

"I worked that out for myself, thanks. What kind of list?"

"It's strictly a list of clients I buy from," she said. "Our thief is working from the master list, so when he turns up at someone's house he doesn't know whether he's going to a client I've bought something from or one that I've sold something to."

That was a handy little bit of information. "How did that happen?"

"This file was on my laptop," she explained. "I'd

been working on it, trying to update and better organize it. I'm going to—"

"You know what you should do?" he interrupted her, seeing an opportunity here to assert his authority and to annoy her at the same time. "You should denote those addresses on the map, as well, so that we know whether he's at a buyer's place that can potentially yield a result."

Her brow knitted. "That's exactly what I was about to say."

He knew. That's why he'd said it. First.

He offered her a mildly patronizing smile, payback for her previous preemptive planning, and watched her pretty eyes narrow fractionally with irritation. "Is this place in Valdosta a possible location for the book?" he asked, deciding a subject change was in order.

"No," she said. "This gentleman has a family restaurant and he's bought a lot of things from me to outfit the place. Old washboards and mirrors, bits of farm equipment and cast-iron pots and pans. That sort of thing."

"You probably sell a lot to designers, as well, don't you?"

She nodded. "I do. You'd be amazed at how they can repurpose things. I've got one decorator who bought a cigar cabinet from me and made it into a make-up vanity for a client. And claw-foot tubs installed in courtyards or back porches are getting more popular, as well." She paused. "I actually have mine on my screened-in back porch."

His mouth went instantly dry and his fingers tightened on the steering wheel. *Soft wet skin, sleek dark red hair, pebbled rosy-tipped breasts, a thatch of dark curls between creamy white thighs...*

He needed a moment.

Lex cleared his throat. "You bathe on your back porch?"

"It's not as scandalous as it sounds," she said, her cheeks pinkening prettily. "I have lots of plants both on the porch and around my yard and there's a privacy fence."

Fences could be scaled, and no amount of foliage—unless she'd turned her back garden into a jungle—would keep out determined prying eyes.

"It's nice," she said. "In the winter I fill it up with hot water and soak to get warm and in the summer I switch to cold water to cool down. Each season offers something to enjoy. In the winter I build a fire in my chiminea and sip hot chocolate. When August rolls around, I turn on the ceiling fans and make lemonade, then watch the hummingbirds swarm my feeders."

He had to admit that sounded nice, but he was having trouble thinking about anything other than her wet naked body and what he'd like to do with it. "Your house doesn't have climate control?"

She smiled. "It does, but I like being outside."

"Naked."

Another soft breeze of laughter. "No one can see me, Lex," she said. "It's not like I'm walking down a public street."

He felt a chuckle break up in his throat and more heat pooled in his groin. "No doubt that would stop traffic."

"Elsie would, too," she said.

He grimaced dramatically and swore. "Thanks for putting *that* image in my head. You did that on purpose, didn't you?"

She blinked innocently. "What would make you think that?"

"Because I'm beginning to understand the way your mind works," he said. "And it's just as twisted as your sense of humor."

She nodded primly. "Thank you."

He snorted and shot her a look. "You're enjoying yourself, aren't you?"

"More than I expected," she admitted.

That small remark burrowed into his chest and settled warmly. He glanced at her again, seemingly incapable of not looking at her. He especially liked the smooth skin next to her eyes, the way her lashes curled and cast shadows around them. "You're not what I expected, either, you know."

She rolled her eyes and her lips twisted with droll humor. "Yeah. You expected Elsie."

"It was your name," he admitted. "I just assumed it would—"

"Belong to an old woman," she finished with a sigh. "It's short for Elizabeth. Both my mother and grandmother had the name. My grandmother's was shortened to Liz, my mother's to Beth. My dad wanted me to have the name, but use a different variation thereof, so I became Bess."

"It suits you," Lex told her, knowing it was true. "It's different and old-fashioned. You don't hear it often anymore."

"I can't believe Brian didn't tell you," she said.

It was so bizarre hearing her use Brian's given name. Lex imagined his wife, whom he'd only met briefly, called him that, but Jamie, Guy, Huck, Will and the rest of the guys all called him Payne.

A bark of laughter came from his throat. "Oh, it wasn't an oversight," he said, shooting her a look. "It was a joke and it was on me."

"Ahhh," she said, comprehension dawning. "You jumped to the wrong conclusion and, rather than him clearing it up, he just let you keep thinking it." Her smile turned admiring. "Score one for Brian."

"You don't have to sound so impressed."

She shrugged helplessly. "Maybe not, but I am."

"Security agent doubling as entertainment." He sighed. "That's a sorry state of events right there."

"It's working for me," she said, looking out the window once again.

He chuckled and shook his head. Then that made two of them, Lex thought. Because he was having entirely too much fun. And if she wanted him to *really* entertain her, then he'd be more than happy to oblige.

Although he imagined *Brian* wouldn't appreciate that at all.

Lex was supposed to be catching a potential thief and finding a Wicked Bible, not getting to know Bess Cantrell in the wickedly biblical sense.

But he seriously doubted that was going to stop him. The tug between them—the sheer magnitude of the attraction—was simply mind-boggling. Utterly out of the realm of his experience. Her very breath resonated deep within him, making him aware of the rise and fall of her chest, the steady beat of her heart, every bit of air that moved between her lips. It was need in its purest form, distilled into something so potent he could scarcely think for being aware of her.

He was doomed, Lex thought, and looking forward to his own destruction.

"HE HASN'T BEEN HERE," Chester Herman said hours later when they'd arrived in Valdosta. "I've been looking for him, too," the older gentleman told them.

Bess tried not to show her dismay, but had to admit she was feeling damned disappointed. She'd been certain that Bastard was going to show up at Chester's.

She accepted the cup of coffee Chester offered her and took a seat at his kitchen table. She smelled fresh bread in the oven and a hickory fire burned merrily in the small cast-iron stove, spreading a cozy warmth through out the room.

Lex had taken her map and lists and, at Chester's nod, spread them on the table to review them himself. Though it was ridiculous, she found herself smiling when she saw his lips moving as he read. Of course, she'd be interested in what his lips were doing regardless, because she loved everything about them, was utterly fascinated by them.

The overhead light cast a bright glow on his face, illuminating one cheek in harsh relief and creating a shadow beneath. She followed his jawline with her gaze and lingered over his neck, the masculine strength she saw there. She wanted to kiss that place, to taste the muscles along his throat, and she felt the air thin in her lungs as she imagined doing just that.

He looked up at her then, a smile in his intriguing blue eyes, and she saw a mild bit of satisfaction flash in their depths.

"Want some coffee?" she asked.

He shook his head. "I'm good, thanks."

Rather than continue to stare at him like a kid with her nose pressed against the glass of the candy shop, she turned her attention to Chester.

"Bought anything interesting lately, Chester?"

His eyes twinkled. "Actually, there was something I wanted to show you." He jerked his head toward the living room, then looked at Lex.

Lex gestured to the maps. "I'll be fine in here if it's all right with you," he said. He reached down and absently rubbed a hand over Honey's head. Lex had offered to leave her in the car, but Chester, a dog lover himself, insisted that he bring her in out of the cold.

Chester nodded and motioned her on. Much like her grandfather, the older man had been a widower for almost as long as he'd been married. There were small touches throughout his house where she noticed a feminine influence—doilies on the top of the piano, a pretty floral lamp next to the recliner, the occasional porcelain figurines—but for the most part, Chester had reclaimed the house. He used a fishing bobber for a ceiling fan pull, and the furniture he'd bought had been chosen with an eye toward comfort and not aesthetics.

She knew instantly what he'd added since her last visit and gasped. "A Victrola," she breathed. She walked forward and slid a finger over the smooth wood. "Mahogany, too. Does it play?"

"Like you wouldn't believe," Chester told her proudly. He lifted the lid, then selected a disc, lowered the needle and wound the crank. Bing Crosby's "Sleigh Ride in July" suddenly filled the air and she inhaled, utterly delighted.

"Chester, this is simply extraordinary. Where did you find it?"

"You aren't going to believe this, but at a yard sale."

She felt her eyes widen. "You are kidding me."

He shook his head. "Nope. The couple had found it in the attic of an old house they'd just bought to flip and really didn't know what they had. I picked it for fifty dollars."

"Wow," she said. "That's just incredible."

"According to the serial number, this model was made in 1921 and there were only a little over twenty-thousand produced."

She nudged him in the shoulder. "And you saved it," she said. "If you hadn't come along it would have probably gone to the dump."

"Awww, somebody would have gotten it," he said. "But I daresay I can appreciate it more than most. I can remember my parents having one similar to this, firing it up, pushing back the furniture and dancing around the room."

"That sounds like a wonderful memory," Bess said, touched.

Chester's smile turned reminiscent. "It is."

She offered the older man her hand. "All right, then," she said. "Let's have a go."

He smiled, his faded eyes lighting up, then took her hand and bowed over it. "As you wish," he said, then began to slowly whirl her around the room. She was laughing delightedly when Lex appeared in the doorway, but she waited for the music to stop before giving him her full attention. She'd be willing to bet that Chester hadn't danced since his wife passed away and he'd bought the Victrola because it brought back good memories.

This was why she did what she did, Bess thought.

She dropped into a small curtsy and nodded primly. "Thank you, Chester."

"Thank you, Bess," he returned, his grin sincere.

She looked at Lex once more and watched something curious pass over his face. It was a fleeting look, so quick she thought she might have imagined it. "Did you find something?" she asked.

"How far is Albany from here?"

Bess frowned. Albany? But why would—

"About an hour and a half north," Chester told him.

Shit. She shook her head. "I missed it, didn't I?"

"There are lots of addresses, Bess," he said, trying to make her feel better about the mistake.

She hurried into the kitchen to get her cell phone.

"I'd better call. Did you check to see if that address is on the other list?"

He nodded. "It is."

She swore again, this time under her breath. Dammit, she thought she'd been so careful, thought she'd covered every address. She'd gone over the master list at least three times. How in the hell had she missed Albany? In all likelihood the man they wanted had left Waycross and gone straight to Albany. By now he'd probably been there and gone. She dialed the right number with a sick feeling in the pit of her stomach.

"Mrs. Handley? Bess Cantrell. How are you?"

"I'm just fine, hon. How are you doing?"

"Not too good at the moment." She explained the situation as best she could. "He hasn't been there, has he?" she asked.

"I'm afraid so, dear. He's been gone about an hour. Said he was working with you now and that you'd sent him on the road, that you'd gotten into the rare books business and were looking for an old Bible. He even showed me a picture of it."

Bess massaged the bridge of her nose. "He didn't hurt you or try to bully you, did he, Mrs. Handley?"

"No," she said. "He wasn't what I'd call friendly, but he wasn't rude, either. Mostly he just seemed to be in a hurry. When he saw that I didn't have the book, he thanked me for my time and left rather abruptly."

So she hadn't had it, Bess thought, wilting with relief. Whoever had the book needed to be made aware of its worth and that person should be the one to profit from it, not some jerk who was trying to hoodwink them out of it. "Did you happen to catch his name?"

"I did. He said his name was John Smith."

She smirked and looked at Lex. "John Smith, eh?"

"That's right. Plain name for such an odd-looking fellow," she remarked.

Bess's antennae twitched. "Odd-looking how?"

"Well," she said, "he had one blue eye and one brown eye and was wearing a really bad hairpiece."

"Anything else?" Bess prodded.

"His fingernails were dirty," she said matter-of-factly. "I should have known he didn't work for you. Should have known better than to think you'd work with anyone who had dirty nails."

Bess smothered a laugh. "Hygiene is important," she said. She pressed the older woman a little further, but didn't come up with anything more than what they'd already learned. When she disconnected, she filled Lex in on everything. "Mrs. Handley says that she'd put him in his mid to late forties, that he had one blue eye and one brown eye—"

"Heterochromia," Lex said, surprising her with the

medical term. She knew it, too, but only because her grandfather had explained it to her after she'd seen a child with the same anomaly.

"—and that he was wearing a bad rug and had dirty fingernails."

Lex frowned. "Dirty fingernails? That's an odd thing to notice."

She grinned. "That's Mrs. Handley."

Evidently still pondering that, Lex consulted the maps again. "He should be coming here next." He winced. "Unless he moves on into Alabama. There are several contacts close together over there."

Bess tapped a finger against her chin. "I can't believe he'd skip coming here. He's too close."

"He could have missed it," Lex said.

"Possibly."

"You're welcome to hang around here and wait on him," Chester told them.

She could tell that Lex was torn. He consulted the maps again, then absently rubbed his shoulder. That was the second time she'd seen him doing it since they'd arrived. The spot where he'd been shot, she suddenly realized, her heart giving a squeeze. It must be aching. Even though she imagined it would bug him that she'd noticed—men and their crackbrained ideas of masculinity, she thought—she reached into her purse and withdrew a couple of aspirin, then silently handed them to him.

He quirked a questioning brow and she glanced pointedly at his shoulder.

Honey nudged his leg as if to say, "That's the medicine, you fool."

He smiled at the dog, then popped the pills into his mouth and washed them down with a drink of coffee. "Thank you."

She merely nodded. "So what's the plan, boss?"

He grinned. "Oh, you're going to let me be the boss now, are you?"

"Only on a trial basis," she quipped.

Lex glanced at Chester. "If you're sure you don't mind if we hang around for a little while, Chester, then we'll certainly take you up on that. If he's not here in a couple of hours, then I think we can safely assume he's missed this address and has moved on toward Alabama."

"You're welcome to stay as long as you like," Chester told him.

Bess grinned and looked at her old friend. "In that case, I think a little more dancing is in order."

6

IF BESS WAS GOING TO DANCE again, then he was definitely going to get his turn, Lex thought as he and Honey followed Chester and Bess back into the large living room. He took a seat in a wing chair away from the makeshift dance floor and watched as Chester once again fired up the old Victrola. But he'd wait his turn, particularly since Chester looked to be having the time of his life.

Lex had been over the maps and addresses several times and had concluded that the client in Albany had indeed been the only one Bess hadn't included on their map. He sincerely hoped that John Smith—he inwardly snorted at the name—would be here soon so he could take him down, load him up and haul him back to Atlanta, where the boys in blue would take care of him. Theoretically, he and Bess could be home before ten tonight, he could be back in his new apartment, his first assignment completed quickly and competently.

For whatever reason, he didn't think that was going to happen, and there was an even bigger part of him that, perversely, hoped it didn't. Because no mission meant no more Bess and he wasn't ready to say goodbye to her just yet. She was beautiful and interesting and she had a different way of looking at the world—a way that made him appreciate it more—and she was a nurturer and she was...

She was *good,* Lex realized, the simple description fitting her as well as her name. Or as good as a woman with a wicked sense of humor who bathed nude on her back porch could be, he thought, smiling as that little picture leaped obligingly to his mind once more. He shifted, losing room in his pants again, and watched her smile up at Chester, her ripe mouth curling in sultry humor. Take now, for instance.

She'd instinctively known that Chester would want to dance and without batting a lash had asked him. And she'd quietly observed that Lex's shoulder had been hurting and had handed him the pills to make it stop. No muss, no fuss, just a pointed look when he'd played dumb—he knew what the pills were for—and she had gone on about her business, certain that she was doing what she could.

It was that same attitude that had made her so worried over her clients, that made her want to protect each and every one of them like a mama bear protecting her cubs. She knew what was good and true and right and endeavored to achieve that end. That was admirable, Lex thought. And it took character.

Chester laughed as the music drew to a close and gestured to Lex. "You've got to come dance, young man. These old feet have to have a bit of rest."

Lex didn't hesitate. His gaze tangled with hers and he held out his hand. The instant her fingers wrapped around his, he felt something shift in his chest, something so profound he almost hesitated before pulling her into his arms. *Almost* being the operative word there. Wild horses couldn't have dragged him away, he was that damned determined to touch her.

Just *touch* her.

Shaken, he looked down at her and smiled. "This is a nice change," he said. "There wasn't any dancing on the job in the military." He breathed her in, inhaled the air around her and felt it settle into his lungs. She was soft and womanly in his arms, warm and pliant, and he resisted the urge to draw her closer, to mold her more firmly to him.

But this wasn't that kind of dance and Chester, bless him, was watching.

She smelled good, too, Lex thought. Like lemons and something else. Something light and floral. If he leaned forward even the smallest fraction, he could rest his chin on top of her head. He hadn't realized how short she was until that very moment, and something about her petite size beckoned his protective instincts, made him want to hold her closer.

"You're short," he remarked before he thought any better of it.

She looked up at him, droll humor in her eyes. "That's some serious deductive reasoning skills right there," she teased. "What tipped you off? My hair tickling your chin?"

"Yes, actually," he said, looking down at her. The smart-ass. "I like the way your shampoo smells, by the way."

She swept out and twirled beneath his hand, then curled back into his chest and grinned. "It's lemon verbena," she said, her eyes twinkling. "You're welcome to try it."

"No thanks. I'll stick with my manly shampoo and leave the girlie stuff for you."

"Probably wise," she murmured. "It might confuse people if you smelled lemony fresh."

He chuckled softly. "Why do I always feel like you're laughing at me?" he asked no one in particular. "Why do I feel the butt of all of your jokes?"

She pretended to frown. "Who are you talking to?"

"The world," he remarked broodingly, looking down into her lovely green eyes again. She had a tiny mole just to the right of her upper lip, Lex noticed, momentarily concerned because he found that so adorable.

Adorable?

What the hell was wrong with him? What was it about this woman that was completely turning him inside out?

He'd never felt this way about a girl before. Never had this instantaneous level of attraction, fascination and admiration. In fact, he couldn't say that he'd ever been fascinated by one before. Had never looked at a woman and wondered what she was thinking, or what circumstances shaped her into the person she was today.

But he did wonder such things about Bess, and those unsettlingly original thoughts combined with this ridiculously powerful attraction were making him more than a tad nervous.

Because he wasn't altogether certain he was going to be able to resist her. And he knew enough about women to discern when one was interested in him and, in some twisted trick of fate, she was every bit as hot for him as he was for her.

The lingering looks, the preoccupation with his mouth, the way she instinctively leaned toward him when she was talking, the way she didn't shy away when he lessened the distance between them, the rapid flow of her pulse beneath her skin, the hint of rose on her cheeks. The way her palm tightened around his. Little tells, but tells all the same.

He'd get fired, Lex thought. She was a friend of Payne's, more than a mere client. And this was his first job. It was lunacy to even consider acting on this unholy attraction, and yet in some dark corner of his mind, he knew it was inevitable, that it was going to happen, that it was going to literally rattle his foundation, and knowing that, he couldn't simply let it go.

He had to have her.

In fact, were Chester not smiling now, were he even in another room, Lex knew he would have already made a move. He would have spun her out, and twirled her back in, hauled her up against him and molded that utterly distracting, too-sexy, perpetually smirking mouth to his. He would have memorized every vertebra in her back and measured her waist against his palms. He would have lifted her up and slid her slowly along the front of his body so that she could feel what she was doing to him, and he would have eaten her gasp and tumbled her onto the couch, where he would have systematically removed her clothes and buried himself in her softness.

"Lex," she hissed.

He blinked stupidly down at her.

"The song is over," she said, looking gratifyingly flustered and short of breath. She backed carefully away from him, and it was only then that he realized that he *had* hauled her closer to him. Close enough for her to feel what she did to him, to confirm any mere suspicions she might have had.

Brilliant, Lex thought, mortified.

Still beaming at them and completely oblivious to the massive hard-on Lex was trying to get under control, Chester clapped enthusiastically from his chair. "Well done," he cried. "Oh, well done!"

He'd done it all right, Lex thought. And there was no *un*doing it now.

THREE HOURS LATER, WHEN IT was obvious that Asshole Bastard aka John Smith wasn't going to show up, Bess, Lex and Honey loaded themselves back into Lex's SUV.

"Well, hell," Lex said as he cranked the motor.

She knew. Well, hell, indeed. "Do you think he missed this address?" she asked. "Or do you think he might have caught wind that we're after him and he's changing up his strategy?"

With a final wave at Chester, Lex aimed the car down the drive. "I don't know. He probably knows that you're calling people because at least one of them—Gus, was it?—was ready for him. Would he assume that you were chasing him or had gotten someone else to do it?" He released a breath. "I don't know. I do know that I'm hungry, so I think our first order of business is to find somewhere to eat and then we'll plot our next move."

"I don't want to leave Honey in the car," Bess said, shooting a look at the sweet dog. Honestly, the way Lex's dog followed his every move was nothing short of incredible. Honey didn't just love Lex— she was intensely protective of him. If Lex moved, Honey moved. For whatever reason, she'd appointed herself his guardian and took the job very seriously. That sort of devotion was hard to ignore and Bess knew the animal would be miserable locked in the car away from Lex.

Lex's smile was grateful. "Thanks," he said. "I don't like leaving her in the car, either. She gets anxious."

She'd noticed. "It's not a problem. We can go to a drive-through and pick up something or maybe find a hotel with room service."

She'd expected this to take several days and had packed accordingly, but somehow when she'd considered being on the road with one of Brian's security experts for several days, she hadn't considered that she might be attracted to him. Or that he might be attracted to her.

She'd sensed his interest from the start, had watched it flare in his eyes a couple of times and would even go so far as to say they'd flirted quite shamelessly with one another. But sensing it and feeling it were two entirely different things....

And she'd felt it.

High on her belly.

That unmistakable nudge, the thick ridge of his blatant, panty-scorching erection.

Mercy.

She *wanted*. More than anything, she just *wanted*. She wanted to kiss that unbelievably carnal mouth, to know how his lips felt against her own. She wanted to slide her hands all over his body, to feel his skin beneath her greedy palms, mapping his warm flesh. She wanted to kiss his injured shoulder and nibble her way along his neck. She wanted to kneel behind him and rake her aching nipples across his back and listen to him hiss with pleasure, with wanting. She wanted to watch his eyes darken and droop, to feel his powerful fingers sliding over her rib cage and curving along her hip and to feel them in darker places, hidden places she instinctively knew he'd expertly explore.

She wanted to slip her fingers into his hair while he fed at her breasts and feasted between her legs and she wanted to welcome him into her body with a sigh dredged from her very soul. She wanted him to take her long and slow and then hard and fast and every variation in between.

She. Wanted.

And this need, this ache, this desperation, was so out of the realm of her understanding she didn't even try to make sense of it. There was no point.

There were half a dozen legitimate reasons this shouldn't happen between them, why they shouldn't act on this attraction. In the first place, they were supposed to be catching a criminal bent on harassing her customers. In the second place, he was Brian's friend. In the third place, this was his first assignment. For all she knew he could lose his job over an affair with her.

And, perhaps even more importantly…she didn't do this kind of thing.

She didn't fall into bed with men she'd just met. In fact, she could count her sexual partners on one hand. On two fingers actually. She'd never been much of a dater. Before her grandfather had died she'd spent all of her time with him, and then later, after he'd passed away, she just hadn't wanted to bother. She knew that sounded terrible, but Bess had her reasons. Or *reason,* rather.

People were fleeting, she'd learned. People left. People died. People moved away. People lost interest. People weren't dependable.

But things were, which was why she'd devoted her life to finding them.

She knew her reasoning wasn't rational—Lord knows Elsie had told her often enough—but Bess was happy with the way things were. If she didn't love someone, then she didn't have to worry about them dying, or leaving, or not loving her back. And she was perfectly content on her own.

Or she always had been.

Her gaze slid to Lex and a sort of horrible, inevitable furious despair welled up in her chest, momentarily preventing her from breathing.

Honey leaned in from the backseat and nudged her shoulder, startling her, and Bess breathed a sigh of relief and slipped a hand over her soft head.

If she followed her wayward libido and wound up in bed with Lex, she had an awful feeling she was going to get tangled up in more than the sheets. She'd known from the instant she'd looked at him that he was going to be…something. Special? Maybe. Trouble? Definitely. She'd known him less than a day—*a day*—and already her heart gave a little melting leap of affection every time she looked at him.

That couldn't be normal.

But she couldn't deny it all the same. Honestly, it was almost as if a part of her had recognized him from the start, some hidden consciousness had labeled him familiar and known. As though her very soul had looked at him and said, "Hello, old friend, it's been too long."

Ridiculous. But the sensation was very strong and equally real.

Just like the longing currently chugging through her veins. It, too, was powerfully authentic and she wished she could do something to lessen its effect because she was literally ready to squirm in her seat. The core of her sex pulsed with every rapid beat of her heart and her breasts ached and pebbled behind her bra. She curled her toes in her shoes and tried to concentrate on something different. She silently sang "Yankee Doodle Dandy" and then moved on to the "Battle Hymn of the Republic." When that didn't work, she started conjugating Latin verbs. *Amō, amās, amat...*

She swallowed a moan. Naturally she chose *love*.

Lex pulled to the end of the gravel drive and, instead of turning right, shifted abruptly into Park. He muttered a hot oath, then turned, slipped a hand along her jaw, into her hair and angled her mouth for his kiss.

He didn't ask permission, he didn't hesitate and he didn't hold back.

Hallelujah.

It was *the* most thrilling kiss she'd ever gotten in her life and it didn't have anything to do with the fact that he was damned good at it, that his mouth was the sexiest thing she'd ever seen or that she'd been thinking about sliding her tongue across it since the first moment she'd seen him.

It was because he wanted it as much as she did,

because he'd been craving the same damned thing for as long as she had and because he simply couldn't help himself.

He *had* to kiss her.

That's what made it the best. *His* longing, *his* wanting, *his* desire.

And what woman didn't want that?

He made a low groan in his throat and thrust his tongue more deeply into her mouth, sliding it against her own. His hands were huge and warm, his fingers softly kneading her scalp as he fed at her mouth, and if she'd thought her panties were moist before, they were positively drenched now.

She turned more fully, aligned herself as well as she could, given the high console between them, and pushed her hands into his hair. It was soft and sleek and felt cool beneath her fingers. She slipped her thumb along the muscle beneath his jaw, savoring the feel of it, and deepened the kiss, sucking his tongue into her mouth.

He wrapped his arms more fully around her, his hands sliding along her back, around her rib cage. *Up!* she thought desperately as she felt his thumb skim beneath the underside of her breast. Her breath stuttered out of her lungs and into his mouth and he inhaled it greedily, couldn't seem to get enough of her.

And she knew exactly how he felt because she'd

been thinking about this kiss—yearning for it—all day, and even though that wasn't exactly a particularly long time, it had felt like forever. Every second preceding their kiss had been like a pregnant pause, a permanent prelude, a miserable eternity and now...

Now it was happening and it was even better than she could have imagined. He didn't just kiss, he made love with his mouth, and his lips—his lips were positively lethal. She sank farther into him, drooped so that his hand finally found her breast, and the sensation was so exquisite it ripped the breath from her lungs.

She—

A horn suddenly blared impatiently and they sprang apart, Honey barking at the car behind them, almost in admonition.

Breathing deeply, Lex swore and seemed to be gathering patience from a higher source, an exercise she fully understood because she was pleading on her own behalf, as well.

"There," Lex said after a moment, as if they'd just taken care of something important. He dropped the gearshift back into Drive and took off. "Do you feel better?"

Bess thought about it. "Only in the sense that I want to tear your clothes off and do bad things with you," she answered honestly.

Because at this point, what was the real benefit in

lying? In playing coy? She'd practically thrust her breast into his hand. Had practically poured herself into his lap. He knew she wanted him. Hell, it wasn't like it was a secret.

He turned to look at her, his lush mouth slack, and the tires whined as he momentarily veered off the road. With a jerk, he corrected quickly and swore again.

"You're going to get me fired," he said, as though it was a foregone conclusion.

"Don't worry," she said, laughing softly. "I'm friends with your boss."

7

SHE WANTED TO TEAR HIS clothes off and do bad things with him?

Lex felt his blood pressure race toward stroke level. Did she have any idea what her very honest, unbelievably wicked answer was doing to him? How much he wanted her to explain "bad things" in detail to him. In that lovely voice with that especially sexy mouth?

He couldn't walk into a hotel looking like this, he thought with a futile glance at his crotch. He was *indecent*. He was practically coming out of the top of his jeans, was in very real danger of *coming* in them, as well. He hadn't had a misfire like that since he was in junior high, and one comment from her— one loaded remark—and here he was, his launch sequence initiated, detonation imminent.

He swore silently and tried to concentrate on

something other than the feel of her breast in his hand, the taste of her mouth against his. Warm and soft, yielding and then laying siege. She was amazingly responsive, had come alive in his arms and been every bit as desperate and relieved that he'd kissed her as he had himself.

Major turn-on.

And he'd been "on" for hours already.

He wished that he could regret kissing her, that he could even admit he'd made a mistake…but he couldn't because he didn't regret it, mistake or not. He'd been thinking about her mouth—wondering what she'd taste like, how she'd feel, how she'd kiss— all damned day and, after dancing with her, touching her, well…he'd been done for. They'd left Chester's and all he'd been able to think about once they got into the car was how her lips looked when she smiled, and then he'd *snapped*.

He'd had to kiss her.

Had felt like his organs were going to vibrate right out of his body if he didn't, he was so strung out with desire. He'd been horny before, knew what lust was, and this was no garden variety. This went well beyond mere wanting. It was a craving, an obsession, a hunger he couldn't satisfy, and he knew with the very small rational part of his brain that wasn't consumed with diving dick-first into her that he was in way over his head. The lust he could explain away—

she was beautiful and sexy and intriguing—but those other emotions, the softer ones, the ones he'd never felt before... they were going to get him into trouble.

She was trouble.

Her cell suddenly rang and, seemingly grateful for the distraction herself, she quickly withdrew it from her purse and answered. "Evening, Elsie," she said. "Is everything okay?"

From the corner of his eye he saw her frown. "Elsie, what did I tell you? Didn't I tell you to only call me if it was important?" She paused and her nostrils flared with irritation. "Elsie, I am not in danger. I'm with Lex and we're—" She flushed. "Elsie, you're being ridiculous. I'm perfectly safe. Yes, yes, your sight." She sounded exasperated. "I wish your sight would have told us that John Smith was going to avoid Valdosta. It would have saved us a trip." Another pause then, "No, we're going to head toward Alabama. We think he's going to go that way next." She darted him a look. "Not that it's any of your business, but yes, I'll have my own room." Her expression blackened. "*Elsie.* I've got to go. Call me if anything *important* comes up." She disconnected and muttered a curse. "Honestly," she said. "Her and that damned sight."

Lex grinned. "What's she predicting this time?"

"She's not really predicting anything, but she

keeps telling me that she's getting a premonition that I'm in danger. She keeps seeing a gun."

The back of his neck prickled with unease and a sick sensation settled in his stomach. Remembered pain shot through his shoulder and his mouth parched. "A gun?"

"Yes. And to her it means I'm in danger."

"From what?" he asked.

She flushed again and pushed her hair out of her face. "Well, before it was just a vague sense of impending doom, but now she's decided that it's coming from…you," she finished on a little exhale.

He felt his eyes widen. "Me?" he repeated. "Why am I supposed to be dangerous?"

"I don't know," she said, though he got the impression that she wasn't being completely truthful. "But it's just ridiculous. If I had a dollar for every time she's predicted my bogus fortune I could give John Smith the hundred grand and we'd save ourselves a helluva lot of trouble."

"True," he said. "But we'd be missing all this fun."

The comment had the desired effect. It startled a laugh out of her and he felt her relax, watched the tension ease out of her shoulders. "Thanks," she said. "I needed that."

It was ridiculous how much that little smile he'd coaxed from her meant to him. "No problem," he told her. He paused as a thought struck. "I'm going to check in with Payne," he said, shooting her a look.

"Sure," she said. "I imagine he likes being kept in the loop."

Payne answered on the second ring and Lex quickly brought him up to speed, leaving out the bit where he'd kissed Bess. That really wasn't relevant to the case, he told himself, more than fully aware that he was splitting hairs and putting off the inevitable. If this went where he thought it was going—directly into bed—then there was no way in hell he'd be able to keep that from his boss. It was dishonest, and he'd own it and take his lumps before he'd be mistaken for a liar.

"Listen, do you have any contacts within the DMV?"

"I don't need them," Payne said. "What do you want?"

"Our guy is in his mid-to-late forties, is partially bald and has one brown eye and one blue eye. If you could search the records—"

"On it," Payne said. "I'll email you every guy who might fit the description."

"Thanks," Lex told him. "Oh, and one more thing. He has dirty fingernails. I'm thinking he might be a mechanic, someone who can never quite get the oil off his hands."

He heard Bess gasp beside him and she smiled and

nodded her approval. He might as well have achieved world peace for all the pride that swelled in his chest. He was losing his freaking mind. Definitely, definitely losing his mind.

Sheesh.

"Noted," Payne told him. He paused. "So what did you think of Bess? Was she everything that you expected?"

"Oh, I think you knew exactly what I was expecting," Lex told him.

Payne chuckled. "Sorry," he said. "I know I should have corrected you, but I just couldn't resist the joke. McCann is rubbing off on me."

"I mistook Elsie for her," Lex said, shooting Bess a look from the corner of his eye. He saw her smile and that gentle quirk of her lips hooked a spot right in his chest and tugged.

Payne laughed harder this time. "Elsie is something else."

"That's one way of putting it," Lex said.

"Did she make any predictions?" he asked. "She has the sight, you know." There was a smile in his voice.

No, but she'd rattled his cage. When she'd made that you've-come-close comment, he knew she'd been talking about his near-death experience and it had unnerved the hell out of him. He didn't talk to anyone about that—wouldn't even discuss it with the shrink they'd made him see in the military, and she'd held his hand and…

"I know you think she's off her rocker, but she gets it right every once in a while," Payne said. "She told me that Emma was pregnant the first time before Emma even knew it herself."

"Really?"

"Yeah."

"She could have simply made a good guess."

"She could have," Payne agreed, but it was obvious that he didn't believe that. It was hard to imagine the cool, levelheaded Specialist believing in a half-baked psychic like Elsie, but if he did, then there had to be some merit to her gifts.

Was Bess really in danger then? Lex wondered. Was their guy carrying a gun? Or was that simply more of Elsie's melodrama? A nudge of dread prodded his belly and some epiphany dangled right out of his grasp, fleeing before it was fully formed.

Promising Payne he'd look for that email and that he'd check in tomorrow, Lex ended the call.

"He's not going to fire you over me, you know," Bess told him, looking somewhat smug.

"Oh?" He didn't think so, either. He and Bess were both consenting adults, and as long as their relationship didn't interfere with the job he needed to do, he really didn't see it being a problem. But he wondered what made her so sure.

"Have you ever met Emma?" she asked.

"Just once. She seems like a great girl."

"She is," Bess confirmed. "Do you know how he met her?"

"No."

"On a job, much like this one."

He swiveled to look at her, mildly stunned. "Really?"

"And Huck? He was actually supposed to be guarding Sapphira." Her lips curled into a knowing smile. "And surely you've heard the story about Jamie and Audrey?"

He knew that Jamie had married Colonel Garrett's granddaughter, but wasn't aware of the circumstances that had brought the marriage about. He hummed under his breath. "I haven't heard the official story," he said.

She grinned. "Well, suffice it to say that Audrey's grandfather knew that Jamie had a bit of a reputation as a player and sent Jamie up there to flirt with her enough to keep her from becoming engaged to a man her grandfather didn't like."

He whistled low. "You're kidding me."

She shook her head. "No, I'm not. He was supposed to instill doubt, that was all, but things obviously went a little further than her grandfather anticipated," she concluded with a significant nod.

That was for sure, Lex thought, still trying to

absorb everything that she'd told him. Impressed, he turned to look at her. "How do you know all of this?"

She shrugged. "I told you already. Brian's a friend."

He pulled into the parking lot of a popular hotel chain he knew would have room service, turned to look at her and grinned. "And you don't think he'll fire me, huh?" he asked, his voice low.

She shook her head. "No, I don't."

He bent forward and kissed her again, sighed against her mouth as heat licked through his veins once more. His heart swelled right along with another organ. "In that case...I'm going to let you tear off all my clothes and do bad things with me."

BESS WAS A QUIVERING PILE of goo by the time they made their way to the room, Honey trotting ahead of them down the hall. Thankfully this was a pet-friendly hotel and the clerk had even offered the dog a treat when she'd handed over the key.

Lex inserted the card into the lock, then opened the door and held it for her as she moved past. The room was bigger than she'd imagined with a king-size bed, a low dresser and flat-panel television. A small dining table was positioned in front of the heavily curtained windows and a desk with a roll-ing executive chair completed the furnishings, which were dressed in warm golds and jewel tones. A peek into the bathroom revealed a very large tub and a nice vanity area.

Lex made a moue of approval. "This is better than I expected."

Bess, too. "This certainly beats the subpar chains I normally frequent when I'm on the road," she told him.

He stilled as though that thought had never occurred to him. "How often are you on the road?"

"At least a couple of weeks out of the month," Bess said.

"Alone?"

She plopped down on the edge of the bed and toed her shoes off. She grinned. "Of course." She shot him a look. "I can't very well take Elsie with me." She grinned. "In addition to being miserable, I'd have no one to look after the store."

He grimaced, but didn't say anything, which was just as well. But she knew what he was thinking because her grandfather had thought the same thing—it wasn't safe. To which her standard reply was always "Hogwash." She had a cell phone, she had her GPS so she was never lost and she had her van serviced once a month to make sure that everything was in good order.

She'd had the occasional flat—she invariably picked up a nail at some point or another, particularly if she got too close to an old barn—but she knew how to change a tire. And, in the event she ever got into any trouble she couldn't handle, she kept her pistol beneath the front seat.

"Have you ever thought about getting a dog?" Lex asked. "Good company and a little protection. I'm of the opinion that every person should have a pet of some sort."

She had, actually, but didn't know when she'd have time to train an animal. After a moment, she said as much. "I'd love to have a dog," she told him. She smiled warmly at Honey. "Especially after watching you with her. She's very protective of you, constantly putting herself in front of you."

"I know," he said, rubbing the dog's head. "She's a good girl, aren't you, Honey?" he murmured, bending down closer to the canine, who lapped up his affection.

She wouldn't mind lapping up his affection, too, Bess thought, desire pinging her middle once more. *I'm going to let you tear off all my clothes and do bad things with me,* he'd said, his voice low and husky with the promise of sin.

He looked up at her and his blue eyes darkened with desire. "How do you feel about postponing dinner?"

So long as she could make a meal of him first, she didn't give a damn. "I'm in favor of it," she said, releasing a stuttering breath as her gaze fastened on his mouth once more, silently communicating what she really wanted.

Lex grinned and stood, then came forward and tumbled her back onto the bed. He was big and hard and wonderful and she relished the feel of him, the weight of him against her. His hands found her face, his thumbs sliding along the underside of her jaw, then he angled his lips over hers and kissed her. Sweet joy bolted through her and she turned, pressing herself more firmly against him.

Good heavens, this was crazy. This need, this desire. It utterly consumed her, made her want to simultaneously laugh and weep. She rolled him onto his back and straddled him, then found the hem of his sweater and tugged. The first feel of his bare skin beneath her hands made her moan with pleasure—so warm, so sleek—and she carefully worked the fabric up and out of the way, slowly revealing the beautiful landscape of his chest. Muscled abs, flat male nipples set on a slant against magnificent pecs, soft whorls of dark brown hair.

Mercy.

Though she knew he wouldn't appreciate the adjective, *beautiful* was the first word that leaped to mind. In a purely masculine way, of course.

He leaned up so that she could tug the sweater completely out of the way and she let her gaze drift over his exposed skin, eating him up with her eyes. Her heart gave a hard squeeze when she spied the mangled scars on his shoulder, the puckered, shiny skin, and she bent forward and kissed them, lingering there while she slid her hands back down his belly and found the snap at his jeans.

He gasped and she wasn't sure if it was because she'd kissed his scars or because she'd reached for his zipper, but something told her it was the former. Was he ashamed? she wondered. Embarrassed by the evidence of his wound? If so, then she desperately wanted to correct his thinking. His scars were a badge of honor, proof that he'd fought for their country and survived. It humbled her in a way she hadn't anticipated, made him even more dear, more…everything.

Seemingly not content to be the only one without a shirt on, Lex carefully tugged hers out of the way, as well. She leaned back and let him look at her, loving the way his eyes went all heavy-lidded and sleepy looking. It made her feel beautiful. Wanted. He reached up and fingered the lace on her bra. "Pretty."

"Thank you," she said.

He popped the front closure and her breasts almost sprang free, the fabric catching on her nipples. He bent forward and nudged the lacy cup aside with his nose, then nuzzled her breast, his hot mouth—*oh, that mouth,* she thought as a delicious shiver moved through her—fastening around the pouting nipple.

She gasped and framed his face with her hands, felt the hot length of him press up against her, but it wasn't enough because they weren't naked and he wasn't inside her. And suddenly, that's all she needed, all she wanted. Her heart raced in her chest and frantic blood pounded in her ears. Her body was both strung out and languid and she wanted him, desperately needed him more than she'd ever needed anything in her life.

Though she'd never felt more alive, conversely she was certain she was going to die if he didn't take her, if he didn't get inside her.

She squirmed against him once more and felt him buck beneath her. The next instant he'd rolled her onto her back, was working his way down her belly, that warm mouth making a sensational trek over her ribs, around her navel. He unbuttoned her jeans and she heard the zipper whine as he lowered it, then he slid his big hands over her hips and swiftly removed them, panties and all.

Bare, but feeling far from exposed, Bess leaned back against the bed and felt his hot gaze travel over her. She liked the way it made her feel—wicked and wanton and depraved. He pulled his wallet from his jeans, then determinedly snagged a couple of condoms and tossed them on the bed. Five seconds later he'd shucked his pants and donned the protection and was nudging her folds, poised at her entrance.

He bent forward and kissed her again, his eyes dark, his mouth wonderful against hers and she arched up, slickening him with her own juices.

He groaned and pushed forward.

Lights sparkled as her vision went black and she inhaled sharply as he filled her up. He took every bit of room inside her, stretching her until she could feel every inch of his hardened flesh.

Every vein, every ridge, every ripple, every bump.

She could feel him pulsing inside of her, his very heartbeat in her core, and something about that simply did it for her, literally lit her up inside, and she tightened around him and rocked her hips.

He smiled above her, that unbelievably carnal mouth curling with masculine satisfaction, and she slid her hands up over his chest, up his neck and into his hair, where she pulled him down to kiss him again. His tongue plunged in and out of her mouth and his hips mimicked the action, in and out of her body. She met him thrust for thrust, anchored her legs around his waist and rocked against him.

Her heavy breasts bounced on her chest as he pushed into her, her aching nipples abraded by his masculine hair, the combined sensation making the tingling in her womb intensify. He threaded his fingers through hers and anchored their hands over her head, stretching her out, then took a breast into his hot mouth once more, suckling her deeply.

Her eyes literally rolled back in her head.

He shifted then, angling higher, where every long, delicious stroke of his body into hers nailed that sensitive place at the top of her sex, making it swell, hum, tingle and burn.

Oh, heaven help her. She was— Almost— Ohhhhh, damn.

One moment she was lost in the perfection of their joined bodies, the way his hips fit almost providentially in the cradle of her thighs, and the next she was flying apart, splintering into a million pieces.

Her breath lodged in her throat, her mouth opened in a soundless gasp and then she moaned, a long keening cry that felt like it had been ripped from her very soul. She couldn't catch her breath, couldn't escape him, and the pleasure intensified with every push of his magnificent body into hers. Her body went rigid as she rode out the wave of climax, relishing every ebb and flow of the singular sensation, then she went limp, sated and replete.

Elsie had been right, Bess thought dimly. She was definitely in danger...but it was her heart that was at risk.

8

Do BAD THINGS WITH YOU, indeed, Lex thought as he pushed deeper and deeper into Bess's sweet, extraordinarily responsive body. Her pink-tipped breasts bounced on her chest, absorbing the force of his thrusts, and her hips, soft and womanly and flared just so, rocked beneath his, taking him in, a perpetual invitation into her body.

If he'd ever felt anything as perfect as Bess—as the two of them together—then he couldn't recall it. Every cell in his body responded to her on a primal, visceral level, and though he'd never felt this way about a woman before, he was consumed with the idea of branding her forever, of making her his. Had he been a caveman he would have clubbed her over the head, then dragged her by the hair back to his cave, where he would have kept her forever and defended her at all costs.

He could taste her on his tongue, smell her in his nostrils—sweet and musky and laden with the scent of their sex. He was breathing her in, even as he moved in and out of her, her greedy muscles clamping around him, squeezing him, loving him with her body.

Her hair, long dark red curls, fanned out beneath her head, and her lips were raspberry-pink and swollen from his kisses. Even now, though he knew he'd satisfied her, she was looking at him as though she were starved for him, as though the rest of the world could crumble down around them, but so long as he was there with her, she'd be fine, she'd be satisfied.

She was a sensual delight, a feast for his senses, and nothing—*nothing*—was more attractive than being wanted, being desired. With every touch of her hands against him, every desperate clutch and release against his dick, every sleepy-eyed look, every sigh and moan, he knew beyond the shadow of a doubt that she wanted him. That she needed him with the same sort of mindless intensity he needed her.

He bent forward and kissed her again, licked a path along her arched throat and dipped his tongue into the hollow of her collarbone, before moving slowly down to lave her nipple, feeling the hardened peak against his tongue. She clamped around him again and the pressure triggered a response in the back of his balls. He angled higher, pushed deeper and upped the tempo.

He felt the first flash of climax kindle in his loins and, seemingly sensing that he was close to release, Bess bent forward and flicked her tongue against his nipple, tasting him as he'd just tasted her. She clamped her small hands on the twin globes of his ass and squeezed, urging him on.

He pounded into her, harder and harder and harder still. The bed rocked beneath them, a roaring built in his ears and the blood rushed from his head to the one farther south. Impossibly, he hardened even more, and then the bottom suddenly dropped out of his stomach—as though he'd just taken an unexpected leap off a cliff—and he came.

Hard.

Sound receded, sensation reigned and her greedy body tightened rhythmically around him, coaxing the orgasm out of him one determined squeeze at a time. He dug his toes into the mattress and lodged himself as deeply into her as he could go, then stayed there until the last of the contractions eddied through him.

He released a shaky breath, then rolled to the side. He made quick work of disposing of the condom, then hauled her up against him and wrapped a hand possessively over her breast. She snuggled deeply into his embrace and a contented sigh rolled between her lips.

"I'm hungry now," she announced, to his immense surprise.

He chuckled and twisted a lock of her hair around his finger. *"Now?"*

She stretched and flexed her toes. "Positively ravenous. Aren't you?"

As if on cue, his stomach rumbled and he laughed. "I guess I am. I hadn't noticed."

"That's because you've been busy doing bad things with me," she said, tracing circles on his chest. It felt nice. Natural, even, lying there with her.

He chuckled. "And enjoying every minute of it." He paused. "I hope you were satisfied."

She laughed, seemingly outraged. "Fishing for compliments? Seriously, I know you saw my eyes roll back in my head." She chuckled. "If that's what you mean by satisfied, then yes, Lex, you satisfied the living hell out of me." She took a deep breath and released it. "Honestly, I'm just glad we got it over with."

He blinked. "What?"

"Well, now we'll be able to concentrate on other things," she explained with some sort of logic he was having trouble understanding. "I've been distracted all day."

As nice as it was to hear that he'd been distracting her all day with his potent sex appeal, he wasn't so sure he liked the way she'd put it. "Got it over with?"

That almost sounded like they weren't going to do it again, in which case he would beg to differ.

And he would beg. Really.

Because once wasn't going to be enough. In truth, he could take her again right now, could feel the tension seeping back into his penis, felt it drift toward her like a damned divining rod.

"You know what I mean. I've been a bit preoccupied with your mouth. Would you hand me the menu? If we don't call room service soon we're going to miss the boat."

Baffled, but flattered, he handed her the folder and she sat up and started blithely flipping pages. She was completely at ease with her nudity, didn't pull the edge of the comforter over her body. And she wouldn't, would she? This was a woman who bathed on her back porch because she had a privacy fence. He was *so* in over his head, Lex thought. And perversely, didn't seem to care.

"My mouth?"

"Oh, man," she said, a frown emerging between her finely arched brows. "I hate it when I get this hungry. Everything looks good, you know? I can't decide if I want a cheeseburger or the chicken and sugared pecan salad. I've been cold today, so something warm would be good, but…"

"My mouth?" he repeated.

"Yes," she confirmed absently, still reviewing her

choices. "It's sexy. The sexiest thing I've ever seen really. I've been thinking about what it would be like to kiss you and how much I'd like to have your mouth on certain parts of my body—my breasts, specifically—and how it would feel against my skin. It's simply—" she gave a delicate shudder "—exquisite."

His felt his expression blank for a second as her words materialized in his mind. *His mouth against her skin, tasting her breasts...*

"What do you want?" she asked, looking up and over at him.

Her. Again. Right now.

She caught his expression and went still, then tossed the menu aside. He was on her in a heartbeat again. Skin to skin, flesh to flesh, his mouth—the one she'd imagined on her breasts—taking a nipple deep into his mouth. She found the other condom he'd gotten from his wallet, tore into the package, then carefully slid it over the engorged head of his penis and rolled it into place.

A moment later she was straddling him, her weeping folds sliding along the thick ridge of his dick, her ripe breasts ready for his lips. Her soft belly, the generous flare of her hips, a thatch of dark red curls at the junction of her thighs. He looked down and saw where they met, saw the tip of his penis peeking out of her sex and almost came again. She leaned up, arching her hips, then tipped forward until she'd successfully guided him to her entrance.

With a slow moan, her eyes fluttering shut and her breath leaking out of her lungs in a long, blissful sigh, she slowly impaled herself on him.

Her hair was long and tangled from their lovemaking and it draped over her shoulders and curled around her breasts, reaching nearly to her waist. She was a sexual vision, a siren, and watching her take him in, watching her enjoy feeling him inside of her, was the single most erotic thing he'd ever witnessed in his entire misbegotten life.

She rested her hands on his chest and worked herself up and down, a gentle, slow deliberate rise and fall. Her breath caught, a low hum of pleasure slipped past her lips, and her eyes, normally a bright vivid green, went dark and verdant. Her teeth sank into her bottom lip and she leaned back, taking him deeper, then she reached around behind her and massaged his balls while she rode him. When she found the sweet spot between the root and sack, he thought he was going to die, to literally expire on the spot.

But he couldn't yet, Lex told himself. He couldn't let her subject him to this sweet torture without repaying it in kind. He bent forward and pulled her nipple into his mouth, suckling hard, then slid his fingers between their joined bodies, found the hard kernel nestled at the top of her sex and stroked it.

She inhaled sharply and rode him harder.

He knuckled her and she went wild, bucking on top of him, stroking the back of his balls, begging him to come with her talented fingers and the sweet friction of her channel.

He left off one nipple and found the other, thrusting upward beneath her, working her clit until a low keening wail ripped from her throat. She leaned forward and rode him with every bit of strength she possessed, harder and harder, her delicious flesh slapping against his as he took everything she had to give. He felt her tighten around him, a prelude to her release, and knuckled harder.

She came for him.

Her body fisted around him over and over, squeezing, contracting, begging him to join her, to let go...

A low groan tore from his throat and she bent forward and caught it, kissing him as he erupted inside of her, spilling his seed into the condom.

Breathing hard, he kissed her again, then rested his forehead against hers. "Let me guess. You're glad we got that over with?"

She smiled against his mouth and he felt her lashes tickle his face. "Immensely."

"THIS IS THE BEST HAMBURGER I've ever eaten in my life," Bess moaned hours later.

"You're just saying that because I've half starved

you," Lex said, dragging a French fry through a puddle of ketchup.

"Yes, but you fed me in other ways," she said, sliding him a look. Ways that she had thoroughly enjoyed. He'd fed a different kind of hunger, one that she knew wasn't going to be satisfied anytime soon. Whether they were compatible in any other way, she knew for certain they were dynamite in bed. They'd come together explosively. And she'd savored the blast.

Having missed room service, they'd showered, then Lex had taken Honey and gone to a local restaurant to get dinner. While he was out, Bess had reviewed the maps again and, even though it was late, had called a couple more of her clients to alert them to the possible threat.

No one had heard from John Smith, which made her more than a tad nervous.

Of course, it could have been that, like them, he'd merely stopped for the night, but she worried all the same.

Finished eating, Lex threw the last bite of his own hamburger to Honey, who ate it gratefully, then he wiped his mouth with a napkin and tossed it on his plate. "I think I'd better check my email," he said. "See if I've got anything from Payne yet."

That reminded her. "I called Mrs. Handley while you were gone and got her email address so that we could forward the pictures Brian sends to you and see if any are a match."

"Mrs. Handley has an email address?" he asked, surprised.

"Doesn't everybody nowadays?"

He bent forward and kissed her forehead. "You are brilliant."

She smiled, pleased. "You'd already thought of it, hadn't you?"

"I had, but that doesn't matter. We have the same goal, after all."

Her lips quirked with droll humor. "I don't re-member you being so open-minded about that this morning."

"That's before I had sex with you," he explained.

If she'd been eating something, she would have choked. "I'm sorry?" she said, shaking her head. "Tell me why that makes sense."

He pulled the laptop from the bag, opened it up and powered it on. The blue screen illuminated his face, making her belly tighten with need again. "It doesn't have to make sense. I'm a man, remember? I only know what I know."

"Ah," she said. "How about I take a crack at it then? Because we've had sex and you've effectively pounded me into submission with your penis, you no longer feel emasculated by my efforts to help?"

He looked up at her, a comically cautious expression on his face. "There's no right answer here, is there? If I say yes, I'm a Neanderthal. If I say no, then I'm a liar."

She merely shook her head. "What am I going to do with you?"

He waggled his brows suggestively. "Bad things?"

They'd already done bad things. Twice. And they still had the rest of the night to get through. Though it was ridiculous—she'd just bared every inch of her body to this man—she felt sort of funny about crawling into bed with him and sleeping. She'd never slept with anyone, ever, even as a child. She'd never had sleepovers or gone to other people's houses and she'd always had a bed to herself. Freakishly, the idea of sharing one with someone was almost more intimate than what they'd just done.

Ridiculous, she knew, but she couldn't help it.

As for her other sexual partners, she'd always been at the guy's house but never spent the night, preferring to go home to her own bed. She'd often heard people talk about spooning and cuddling—romanticizing sleeping in the same bed—but she wasn't completely sure she was going to like it. Once more her gaze slid to Lex, who was deep in concentration. Of course, if she was ever going to like it with anyone, she imagined it would be with him.

Honestly, she didn't know what it was specifically, but something about him affected her on a level she'd never felt before. Was she sexually attracted to him? Her lips quirked. That, she was certain, had been established. But it was more than sex. Much like Honey, she wanted to be closer to him, wanted to listen to everything he had to say. She loved the deep timbre of his voice, the way those beautiful eyes crinkled at the corners when he smiled.

Though she'd barely met him, she knew instinctively that he was an admirable man, that he was good and decent. He was the kind of person who adopted a stray, who smiled indulgently when she danced with an old widower who needed cheering up. A man who would see this job through to the end because he'd said he would. He was smart and funny, unbelievably sexy and gorgeous, and she loved the way she felt when she was with him. As though he held some secret part of her and she was only complete when she was near him.

And if that wasn't dangerous, then she didn't know what was.

Because she didn't want that, ultimately. She didn't want to allow her happiness to get so tangled up in someone that she'd rather die than live if something happened to them.

Like her mother.

Her mother had been so devastated after Bess's father had died that she hadn't wanted to live at all. Bess remembered very little from that time, but she did recall foraging for food in the kitchen while her mother slept. Getting herself ready for school, packing her own lunches, such as they were. Had her clothes been clean? Probably not. But she'd known enough to get herself dressed and outside to catch the bus.

She didn't remember a single tender gesture from her mother after her father died. She'd retreated into the world of her own misery, and other than the scribbled apology at the bottom of her suicide note, she hadn't thought about her daughter.

If that was love, then Bess didn't want any part of it.

Her grandfather had told her later that her mother had always been "fragile." Bess wasn't exactly sure what that was supposed to mean or why it would have made her feel better, but in a strange sort of way, it had. He'd also said she was more like her father and she'd taken comfort in that. In knowing that she was more like the stronger parent.

"All right," Lex said. "There are eight pictures here with names and addresses. If you'll give me Mrs. Handley's email address, I'll forward them to her."

Bess walked over and peered at the faces on the computer screen, trying to discern from their looks which one, if any, was the culprit. There were a couple of really seedy-looking characters, but then she felt bad for thinking that. She didn't know their circumstances or what sort of hand life had dealt them. Who was she to judge based on a photo from the DMV?

She rattled off the address and he sent the file. "She probably won't look at it tonight," Bess told him. "And it's really too late to call."

"Maybe call her in the morning then and let her know the message is there?"

She nodded. That sounded good.

"We'll see what she says before we head out in the morning. If she can ID him, then we can call Payne and find out everything we need to know." He paused and a frown wrinkled his smooth brow.

"Is something wrong?"

He shook his head. "Nothing I can put my finger on, but something about this doesn't feel right."

"What do you mean?"

He grinned at her and shook his head. "That's just it. I don't know. I feel like I'm missing something."

She laughed and quirked a brow. "Developing the sight, are you?"

"Nah," he said. "I'll leave that to Elsie." He paused again and for the first time he seemed a bit nervous.

And then it dawned on her—he wasn't used to sharing a bed with anyone, either, and was every bit as nervous about it as she was. For whatever reason, this heartened her more than she would have believed.

"Wanna see if anything good is on television?" she asked.

He nodded. "I don't suppose you like ESPN?"

"No."

"Damn. You just lost your shot at earning The Perfect Woman title," he teased.

Bess plopped on what she decided would be her side of the bed and aimed the remote at the TV. "I don't suppose you like Britcoms?"

"About as much as having my balls snatched off with red-hot pinchers," he said, startling a laugh out of her.

She heaved a dramatic sigh. "Well, hell. You just lost your shot at earning The Most Forward-Thinking Man award."

Lex slid into bed next to her and hauled her closer to him. She snuggled in and relaxed against him, contented in a way she hadn't expected.

"Perfect women are boring," he said on a sigh, giving her a squeeze.

She smiled. "Forward-thinking men are over-rated."

His chest vibrated beneath her cheek as he chuckled, then the bed shifted and he laughed harder.

She lifted her head to see Honey sprawled on his far side and felt her lips twitch. She should have known that Honey wasn't going to stay on the floor, that she'd want to be by Lex. "Is she jealous or is this a regular occurrence?"

"A regular occurrence. Do you mind?"

"Not at all. If Severus were here he'd be curled around my head right now…with his ass in your face."

"Nice," he said, laughing softly. "I can tell you I'd definitely have a problem with that."

"Cats are clean," she said, stifling a yawn. "In fact, he cleans his ass all the time. I see him do it."

He laughed again, the sound warm and familiar. "Be that as it may…"

She found a sitcom they both agreed on, then she settled more firmly against him, strangely content. And when she awoke the next morning, his chest was bellied up to her back, his arm around her waist, her breast in his hand.

He was definitely a spooner…and she rather liked it.

9

THOUGH HE FELT LIKE THEY should be on the road—should be moving, at the very least—Lex realized there was no point to pressing forward until they knew what direction to head. Bess had called several of her clients last night and, as of this morning, none of them had heard from John Smith. They'd each been asked to call if he did show up, so until the phone rang there was really nothing they could do.

And it was driving him crazy.

Rather than sit inside the hotel room where Bess and the bed seemed to loom large, he clipped Honey's leash onto her collar and told Bess he wanted to walk her for a bit before they got back into the car. That was true, of course, but he also needed to take a minute to get a little perspective, because at some point over the past twenty-four hours, he'd lost it.

Big-time.

This morning he'd awoken with her hair in his face, her sweet rump against his groin and a luscious handful of breast beneath his palm. That had been a first. He'd never physically spent the entire night in bed with a woman. He'd either left hers for his own or sent her on her way. In all honesty, despite the fact that he'd had the most wonderful, mind-blowing, phenomenal sex in his life, something about sleeping with Bess had felt more…significant.

He wasn't altogether certain what was happening to him, but he grimly suspected he was getting increasingly more invested in her than was wise. His head was still a mess from the near-death experience—though the nightmares were fewer and far between, he still occasionally had them—and he'd just started a new job. He didn't have the time to give to a new relationship, even one as sexually satisfying as his and Bess's. He felt like a bastard for even thinking like that. It wasn't like he'd bedded her and wanted to bail.

Just the opposite, really.

He suspected that he'd want to spend more and more time with her, to explore the relationship, and that was a luxury he couldn't afford right now. In addition, though he knew he was going to love working for Ranger Security and anticipated becoming good friends with the men there, he still wanted to do something more. To find that purpose he'd been searching for his whole life.

Being in the military had fulfilled the need somewhat, but not to the extent he knew it should. Did he doubt that his service benefited the greater good? No. And he was proud of his contribution. But he wanted something more. He wanted to do something on a more personal level. He exhaled mightily and watched Honey eye a squirrel with entirely too much interest for his comfort. Lex smiled at his dog. He hadn't been kidding when he told Bess that he thought everybody needed a pet. Honey had certainly been good for his overall mental health. Too bad some of the other wounded soldiers hadn't had the same benefit, he thought, going still at the idea. His heart rate kicked up and his skin prickled, alerting him to the fact that he was on to something special, something that certainly bore thinking about.

But not at this moment. Right now he had to think about Bess and what the hell he was going to do with her.

Or without her, as it were.

And, really, if all of the reasons he'd listed to avoid a relationship with Bess sounded thin and superficial, it was probably because they were. But he had a hard enough time admitting the truth to himself, much less her, so he was going to stick with the superficial excuses for as long as he could.

How could he tell her that he'd been secretly glad to come home? That he'd been terrified of getting shot again? Of dying before he'd truly lived? That he was afraid that when the time came, his fear might keep him from reacting as a man should? How did he know that he wouldn't be a coward?

That was ultimately the problem, Lex realized suddenly.

It wasn't so much that he was afraid to die—it was that he might not be able to act in time to save someone else. How could he confess those things to her when he could barely admit them to himself?

As for what Bess was thinking, who knew? He'd caught her staring at him a couple of times with the most puzzled expression on her face, as though he were a new species or an antique she'd never come across before. In that regard, he imagined that she was every bit as skittish about their newfound attraction as he was. Though she'd been incredibly responsive and open in bed, he'd still gotten the impression that she hadn't had very many partners and, given the fact that she was the most interesting and beautiful creature he'd ever seen, he figured that had to be by choice. So…why? Why hadn't anyone snapped her up? Why was she still single? Her choice?

For reasons that escaped him, he thought yes.

Which naturally begged the question again—why? Why would she *choose* to be alone? Why hadn't she snagged a husband and produced a pair of beautiful children?

Even though he knew it wasn't wise, these were questions he was going to have to find the answers to. He wasn't going to be able to help himself. Much like a crossword, she was a puzzle he desperately had to figure out. He wanted to pick her brain apart and find out what made her tick. Without a quid pro quo, of course.

As for this case, there was absolutely no reason at all why he should be pulling a weird vibe, but he was feeling it all the same. Though he'd been over everything backward and forward and was certain he wasn't missing anything, he couldn't shake the sensation that there was another element waiting to pop out and bite him in the ass. The feeling had him looking over his shoulder and second-guessing his decisions, made him antsy as hell. He was a doer, not a waiter, which Bess had noticed this morning and had teased him about. With that droll quirk of her lips that habitually set his groin on fire, she'd offered to go find him a dragon to slay.

He grinned, unable to help himself. Hell, he'd probably smiled more over the past twenty-four hours than he had in the past six months. And he'd certainly felt more alive, no doubt from the extra blood flow through his body.

Bess came around the side of the building and

waved, then pointed to her cell phone. "We got a call," she said in carrying tones.

Every muscle went tight and he gave a quick tug on the leash to make Honey turn around. "Come on, girl," he said, anticipation making his fingers twitch with excitement. A break, at last.

"Mrs. Handley looked through the pictures this morning and ID'd our guy," she said. "His name is Harold Yeager and he's got a Bluffton address."

He frowned. Bluffton sounded familiar. And if he remembered correctly it wasn't very far from Albany.

"It's about an hour west of Albany," she said.

Lex nodded grimly. "So he went home last night. He's been slowly making the trek back down south and then west."

"I think he must have missed Chester's address," she said. "Otherwise he would have gone there before heading toward Valdosta."

He silently agreed. "I know we need to get on the road, but I want to take a few minutes to do some research on Mr. Yeager," Lex told her.

She nodded. "Of course."

They had just gotten back into the room when her cell phone rang again. Lex pulled his laptop out of the bag and listened as Bess took the call.

"Mr. Johnson? He was? How long ago did he leave?" She smiled, seemingly satisfied. "Thanks so much for letting me know and, again, I'm so sorry about this. Yes, sir," she said. "I'm sure Princess did you proud." She laughed at something the older man was telling her. "You give her an extra treat from me," she said. "Thanks again." She disconnected and looked over at him.

"He was just in Pansey," Bess told him. She hurried over and looked at the map. "Which means that he'll probably go to Ashford next and then on to Dothan."

A few keystrokes later he'd pulled an entire history on Harold Yeager. He smiled and beckoned her over. "He *is* a mechanic," he said, glad that his hunch was right. "He lives in the apartment above his shop. He's forty-three. Recently filed bankruptcy, not married, no dependents. Sells spare parts and yard-sale finds on eBay."

She nodded, impressed, and sent him an admiring glance. "How did you find all this?"

"You'd be amazed at what you can find out about someone on the internet." He studied the map for a moment. "I think we need to skip ahead directly to Dothan and nab him there."

She was still looking at the computer and gave her head a shake. "This is incredible."

He grinned at her and shrugged. "This is nothing. Give me a few more minutes and I could know his credit score, his cholesterol levels and whether or not he's got any overdue books from the library." He popped the lid closed on the laptop and then jerked his head toward the door. "Come on," he said. "We need to get moving. We'll grab breakfast on the road, if that works for you."

She nodded her consent and less than five minutes later they were on their way to Dothan. He still felt something was off, but was glad to be pushing forward. If time hadn't been such an issue, he would have liked to poke around in Yeager's past a little more, see what would motivate the man to try to bully the book out of someone. Something besides the bankruptcy. He'd alert Payne to their new plan and, with any luck, they'd be back in Marietta by nightfall.

His gaze slid to Bess and his heart gave a little lurch at the thought of leaving her, but he beat the sensation back and told himself it was for the best.

And if he kept saying it, maybe he'd actually believe it.

BESS LISTENED AS LEX called Brian and filled him in. The excitement in his voice was practically palpable and his energy literally filled up the car. She didn't know if he was genuinely that thrilled to have a break in the case or if he was just happy to have something else to focus on besides the sudden awkwardness that had sprung up. She wasn't sure what had brought it about since things between them had been so unbelievably effortless and natural—frighteningly so, actually—but couldn't fault him for it when she felt it herself.

It didn't make sense. They'd shared their thoughts, shared their bodies and shared a bed, and yet now...

She wished she understood what had brought the wall up—she'd had no conscious thought of erecting one herself, but knew she had—and didn't know exactly how to take it down. She wanted things to go back to the way they were, when she and Lex had simply been having fun and were hot for one another. The heat was still there—she could feel it burning—but something was getting in the way of the fun.

She couldn't speak for him, of course, but knew where her own anxiety was coming from. She didn't want to think about where this was going, didn't really want it to go any further than where it was right now. If she were completely honest with herself, she'd never felt this sort of breathless anticipation over a relationship before, had never looked at a guy and thought, *I can see myself with him.*

She did look at Lex and think that, and *that's* what was bugging her. The unmistakable knowledge that he was different, that she could inadvertently let him have a piece of her that she didn't want to part with. That she'd just wake up one morning, spooned again, and he'd own her heart.

And, much as she knew that was the fairy-tale

ending, she didn't want it. She couldn't take such a risk. She couldn't let herself become so dependent on him for her happiness that she'd be devastated when he left her, or God forbid, something happened to him. It wasn't worth it to her. Sad? Maybe. But she couldn't help it.

She had her shop and her things and her cat, and really, getting the cat had been difficult for her. She inwardly smiled. But she hadn't so much as *gotten* Severus as he'd gotten her. She'd pulled into a little place in Mississippi, loaded up her van with the things she'd purchased and headed toward the next town. She'd made it onto the interstate before the cat had climbed into the passenger seat, cool as you please, as though he'd been riding shotgun with her for years. The best she could figure, he'd Houdini'ed himself right into her car while the doors were open. Impressed with his ingenuity, she'd been unable to try to find a home for him and instead had made one for him herself.

"We're what?" Lex asked. "About two and half hours from Dothan?"

"That sounds about right," Bess told him.

He pulled into a fast-food restaurant and they ordered a quick breakfast, then got immediately back on the road. "I know we're rushing here," he said. "But I think the timing is going to be crucial."

She agreed. "Did you find out what sort of car he

drives?" she asked, savoring a bite of her sausage biscuit. The coffee wasn't the best—it could strip paint it was so strong—but the sandwich certainly hit the spot. Bess wasn't one of those women who ever "forgot" to eat. If she was late getting a meal, her stomach quickly announced its displeasure.

"Yeah. A black Trans Am. An '80s model with the big golden firebird on the hood."

Her eyes widened significantly. "That should be easy to spot."

He grinned at her, some of the tension easing between them and lessening the strangeness she'd felt inside the car. "Hardly conspicuous, right?"

"What was your first car?" she asked, shooting him a speculative look. "No, wait. Let me guess. A Gremlin."

He choked on a laugh and his eyes widened. "I have not ever driven a Gremlin," he said. "Though I can guarantee you I would have caught action in it if I had."

It was her turn to laugh. "I'm sure you would have caught action if you'd driven a tricycle. You just look like that kind of guy."

She watched him smile again and that grin lightened her heart more than it should have. More than was good for her. *Oh, hell.* "What kind of guy?"

She rolled her eyes. "The kind who was playing train in kindergarten," she deadpanned. "The kind of guy that sneaked kisses behind the school and kept nudie magazines hidden beneath his bed."

He feigned outrage, then gave his head a baffled shake. "Have you been talking to my mother?"

"No," she said, chuckling. "Though I imagine she has many stories to tell."

"I'm sure she does," Lex said, his eyes crinkling with a smile. "My brother and I gave her hell. Or as much hell as my dad would permit, anyway," he added fondly. "My sister was always good, though. Mindful and obedient. Good grades."

They sounded like a lovely family, Bess thought. Norman Rockwell normal, with pretty family Christmas cards and lots of home movies. She almost ached at the thought of it and a miserable yearning burned in her breast. She wished she'd known something similar. Her grandfather had made things as normal for her as possible, but she'd be lying if she said she hadn't missed some of the gentler touches. Someone to braid her hair, teach her about makeup, the birds and bees. She smiled.

Her poor grandfather had taken her to the pediatrician for "the talk" about her cycle and had left it for the nurse to explain. Armed with a box of feminine napkins and a little pamphlet on knowing her body, she'd blushed a million shades of red when she'd walked out of that room and seen him standing there.

He'd turned even redder.

Bless his heart, he'd tried, and he'd given her a good life. Had it been different? Yes, definitely. But it had been good all the same.

"What about you?" he asked. "Any brothers or sisters?"

"No," she told him, knowing that this was moving into territory she didn't want to enter. "Where are you from originally?" she asked.

He frowned, obviously not missing the evasive action on her part. "Blue Creek, Alabama," he said. "It's in the northern part of the state, about thirty minutes from the Tennessee line."

"And your family is still there?"

"My mother, father and sister are," he told her. "My brother is a medic in the army. He's in Afghanistan."

So his brother was still in the service. That must be hard for him, Bess thought. His military career had ended, his brother's was ongoing. Did he envy him? she wondered. She pecked at Lex from the corner of her eye and caught the slight flexing of his jaw, the firmer pressure around those beautifully carnal lips. No, she thought, studying him thoughtfully, envy wasn't the right word. But she wasn't sure what was. Interesting, Bess thought. She wasn't the only one who didn't want to share all her secrets.

"I bet your family worries about him," she said. "Is he older or younger than you?"

"Younger," he told her. "By two years."

Even worse then. Lex had set the example and then he'd been injured and come out. Her heart gave a squeeze at the thought of his injured shoulder. The shiny scars, the marred skin. She couldn't even imagine the sort of pain he'd been in, the horror of what had happened to him. The awfulness of what he'd seen, which somehow made his sacrifice all the more noble.

Though he went to great pains to disguise when he was hurting, she had noticed a few little tells, aside from when he forgot himself and actually rubbed the wound. He would flex his fingers in that hand, give the shoulder a delicate roll and, more interestingly, she'd been aware of this because Honey had alerted her to it. As if sensing his discomfort—his pain— Honey invariably moved closer to him. She'd put her head against his leg, or bump his hand and force a pat. To distract him? Bess wondered. Or to comfort? Probably both.

Her gaze slid to the dog, who was currently resting her chin upon the console, her face next to Lex's arm. Honestly, the relationship between the man and the dog was simply extraordinary. They were utterly devoted to one another.

Bess reached over and petted the dog, rubbed

her velvety ears. "You're a sweet girl, Honey," she crooned.

Lex looked over at her and smiled. "She is," he said. "She saved me."

Saved him? Bess thought, seizing on the extremely revealing comment. Saved him how?

Looking as though he'd like nothing better than to cut his own tongue out with a rusty blade, Lex stared straight ahead. Every muscle in his body had tensed and he looked...braced, for lack of a better description. Braced and miserable. And anything that made him look that unhappy was not something she wanted to ask him about. She couldn't because she knew he'd hate it, because she knew whatever it was would hurt him.

And she wasn't going to satisfy her own curiosity at the expense of his anguish.

She released a deep breath. "You never answered my question," she said.

He slid her a guarded look. "What question?"

"What was your first car?" she reminded him, feigning exasperation. "Honestly, as much as you've been avoiding the question, it must have been something truly horrid." She gasped dramatically. "Ooo, it was a Pinto, wasn't it?"

He studied her for a minute, his mysterious blue eyes boring into hers as though she were a unique and unknown quantity and he was desperately trying to figure her out. She saw relief and gratitude reflected in his gaze and then he blinked and the old Lex was back, confident as ever. "A Pinto? Are you serious? For your information, my first car wasn't a car—it was a truck. A little Chevy S-10, navy blue with a chrome toolbox on the back."

"No doubt it was filled with condoms," she said, rolling her eyes.

His grin turned wicked. "I kept my condoms in the glove box," he said. "Easier access."

Bess cocked her head and looked at him speculatively, then turned and popped open the glove compartment, revealing a large box of ribbed extra-large. She hadn't noticed the ribs, but could vouch for the extra-large. She smirked, shook her head and sighed. "I guess old habits die hard."

He winked at her. "But never unprotected."

10

LEX HAD GOTTEN MANY GIFTS over the years, mostly from his parents and grandparents. He remembered a train set for Christmas one year, birthday tickets to a concert he'd desperately wanted to go to.

But he didn't think he'd ever received anything that he'd appreciated more than Bess's free pass a moment ago. When he'd slipped up and made the "she saved me" comment, he'd immediately regretted it, had known that her keen mind would recognize its significance and her interest would spark.

It had, too. He'd seen it flare in her eyes, watched those pretty green orbs widen with the realization that he'd inadvertently handed her a small nugget of his soul. Any other woman would have immediately asked him what it meant, how the dog had saved him. And would have been perfectly within her rights to do so, because he was the one who'd slipped up and opened the door to the line of questioning in the first place.

But the same mind that had picked up the significance of what he'd said had also recognized that he hadn't meant to say it. No doubt the remark had made her even more curious and yet, rather than ask him about it or insist he explain, she'd changed the subject and let it go.

He'd known from the get-go that she was different, that she wasn't like other women. He'd sensed her unique appeal and that had never been more confirmed than just a few minutes ago, when she'd respected his privacy.

One would think that, in light of her own generosity, he'd repay it in kind...but he wasn't going to. He couldn't help but notice that anytime he asked her a personal question, she immediately turned the conversation away from herself. In fact, she did it with such skill he hadn't even noticed it originally. Which meant that she'd been doing it for a long time, that she had had a lot of practice.

Why? he wondered again, presented with more questions than answers.

Should he press her? No, definitely not. He shouldn't. He should leave well enough alone. In light of the fact that their mission was probably going to be over in just a few hours, that he was going to walk out of her life with no intention of returning, he really didn't have any right to pepper her with questions, to make her fill in the blanks he had about her life.

But, because he was an idiot, because he was a moron, because he simply had to learn everything about her that he could while he had the chance...he was going to.

"Any word from Elsie?" he asked.

"She sent me a text message and told me that 'things weren't as they seemed,'" she said, waving her hands as if the last was supposed to be spooky and mystical. She grunted. "Who knows what that little nugget of vague insight is supposed to mean?"

"I don't know," he said. "But it's funny because I've been feeling the same way. Something seems off about this, but I don't know what it is."

She turned to look at him. "Off? How so?"

He shook his head, almost regretting that he'd given voice to his weird concern. "I don't know," he said. "It's just a feeling. I can't shake the sensation that I'm missing something, that there's more here than meets the eye."

She was thoughtful for a moment and bit her bottom lip. "I don't know what it would be. You've looked at everything. I even handed over a copy of the police report."

"I know," he told her. "It's probably nothing."

"It's probably not," she said. "I'm a firm believer in gut instincts. In heeding intuition."

He was, too, though he definitely didn't think he was psychic.

And while he was heeding gut instincts…

"So you said you inherited your store and your love of 'picking' from your grandfather."

She nodded. "That's right."

"What about your parents?" he asked. "Were they pickers, too?"

She didn't so much as flinch, but he felt her recoil all the same. "No," she said. "My dad was an electrician and my mother was a secretary."

Was? *Oh, hell.* He was a bastard, Lex decided. A horrible, miserable, wretched bastard.

"I'm sorry, Bess. I—"

She swallowed. "They died when I was little," she said. "Eight. My grandfather raised me."

They'd both died? Had they been in some sort of accident?

"He was a widower, was all alone, too, so we ended up being very good for each other."

Still, it couldn't have been easy. Losing both parents at such a young age. And how had her grandfather coped? According to her, he'd been a picker all his life. That meant he'd spent a lot of time on the road. How had adding a little girl to that mix worked? What about school? How had he managed to be gone from home as much as he'd needed and still taken care of an eight-year-old Bess? Had he hired someone?

"So you lived in Marietta the entire time? Went to school there and everything?"

She was quiet for so long he was afraid she wasn't going to answer. "I've lived in the house I'm in now since I was eight," she said. "My grandfather home-schooled me after my parents died, so I didn't get the traditional education, but like to think I got a better one. When I was eighteen I went to college, got my BS in Business, with a minor in English Literature, and lived at home." She sent him a droll look. "I wasn't your average kid. My grandfather knew a *whole* lot about a lot of different things and he shared those things with me. He had a love for dead languages, so he'd make me conjugate Latin verbs while we were on the road. He was a history buff and turned every battlefield into a classroom. Everything he picked had a lesson in it. Where it came from, who made it, why it was important, how it changed the world. That sort of thing."

Even though his mother had been a schoolteacher, Lex was familiar with the homeschooling idea and knew that, for a lot of people, it worked. It obviously had with Bess—she was brilliant—but he couldn't help but wonder about the things she'd missed. Spend-the-night parties, playing sports, playing spin the bottle and going to ball games, time on the playground, commiserating with other classmates about an unfair teacher…those sorts of things.

She waited for him to respond and then chuckled softly. "I've shocked you."

"Not at all," he said, lying with more skill than he knew he possessed. "Your grandfather sounds like an amazing man."

She sighed softly and the ache behind that breath made him want to reach out and touch her. "He was," she said. "There isn't a day goes by that I don't miss him."

"How long since he passed?"

"Three years."

"And you have no other family?"

She shook her head. "None that I'm close to. My parents were both only children, so there weren't any immediate aunts and uncles, no cousins or anything."

Geez, Lord, it just got worse. He couldn't imagine a world without his brother and sister, much less his cousins. Both of his parents had had many siblings and they'd all done their part to go forth and populate the earth. He had at least a dozen first cousins and could vividly remember playing hide-and-go-seek, swinging statue, Red Rover, Simon Says and Truth or Dare with them. He remembered picnics at the park and grilling hamburgers and making homemade ice cream. He remembered the adults getting together and playing cards and Trivial Pursuit into all hours of the night, sending the kids outside to roast marshmallows over a fire. Good times, he thought. Really good times.

Things he'd just realized he'd taken for granted... because the woman sitting next to him hadn't known any of that. He was suddenly hit with the urge to take her over to his parents' house and share his family, to let her be a part of it so that she wouldn't be lonely, so that she'd know what it was like to be surrounded by affection.

They'd love her, Lex thought. And if he wasn't damned careful, they weren't going to be the only ones.

WONDERFUL, BESS THOUGHT. She'd gone from being desired to being pitied. He hadn't had to say a word, but she could sense it all the same. She saw his mouth turn down, watched him silently lament the fact that she didn't have any other family and that she'd lost everyone close to her. Yes, it was true. Yes, she was essentially alone. But she'd learned to be okay with that—this was the hand she'd been dealt and she had no choice but to play it.

But she wasn't going to play it lying down, as it were, and she wasn't going to miss the opportunity to spend at least one more night with him, not if she could help it. Even though she imagined he would say no, she'd decided to take a chance and ask him to spend the night with her. At her house. Where she'd never invited anyone. She didn't want to be poor, pitiful Bess. She wanted to be smart, witty, sexy Bess, the one he couldn't keep his hands off, even when he was asleep.

"I was thinking," Bess ventured.

He chuckled. "That sounds dangerous. About what?"

"Well, we're relatively certain we're about to nab our guy, right?"

"With any luck, yes." He grinned at her. "And I'm feeling pretty damned lucky."

"And it's about a four-hour drive back to Marietta, which will get us back into town late this afternoon."

He nodded slowly. "Right."

She was suddenly nervous, ridiculously so considering what they'd done to and with each other last night. "So, rather than you heading back to Atlanta tonight, I was hoping we could celebrate. At my house. Over dinner."

He stilled, then a slow smile slid over his wicked mouth. "Does that tub on your back porch feature in any aspect of our celebration?"

She grinned, leaned over and kissed his cheek, lingering long enough to breathe him in. "Definitely."

He chuckled low. "Then I'm in."

She hesitated, also wanting to set something else

straight so that there wouldn't be any awkwardness between them come the morning. "Listen, Lex..."

"That sounds ominous," he said. "Do I really want to listen?"

"I think so," she said. "This morning, I think things felt a little off between us and I just want you to know that I know that you've just moved here and started this job." She hesitated. She wasn't quite sure how to finish. "I imagine that you don't have any more time for something serious than I do, and I need you to know that I am not expecting anything beyond a little mutually enjoyable...fun."

A strange expression passed over his face—regret maybe?—but it was gone before she could truly discern it. He laughed, but the sound was forced. "Are you telling me that you want to use me for sex and send me packing in the morning? That you're only interested in my body and not my mind? That you want a no-strings relationship that's going to flare up and burn out with no regrets, no formal attachment, no expectations?"

She considered a moment. Did she want that? Truly want that? No...but it was the most she was willing to let herself have. "That's right," she said haltingly, not sure what to make of him.

He gave a delicate shudder and then smiled. "I feel kind of dirty."

She laughed, relieved. "I'll wash that off of you... in my tub."

He reached over and took her hand, threading his fingers through hers. Her stomach gave a little jump and her pulse leaped in her veins. "I like the sound of that," he said. "Is there room enough for two?"

"Definitely."

He nodded, seemingly pleased, though a shadow still hung around his eyes and she couldn't help but wonder if it was because she'd preempted him by giving him the out. She couldn't imagine that was the case, but hell, who knew? She was fairly certain that, like her, he knew that this—whatever it was between them—wasn't going to have a chance to really go anywhere, but she sensed that, also like her, he almost regretted that.

She smiled softly, more pleased than was truly reasonable.

"You're smiling again," he noted, shooting her a grim look. "Should I be worried?"

"You worry when I smile?"

"It means you're thinking," he explained.

"And that scares you?"

He chuckled. "More than you know."

She could so get used to this, Bess thought. She could get used to being with him like this, listening to him laugh, the easy camaraderie between them.

"Vernon said to park in the back," Bess told him

as he wheeled the car into the drive. She felt a shiver run through her when she realized what they were about to do, but it was a shiver of anticipation and not fear. She wasn't afraid of this asshole, she just wanted to take him down, to make him stop messing with her clients.

He nodded, then slowed the car so that she could get out and let Vernon know they were there. "I'll be right in," he told her.

Having heard them pull up, Vernon opened the door for her. "Ms. Bess, how are you doing? Come on in," he said, smiling warmly at her. "Come on in outta that cold."

She hugged him. "Thanks, Vernon. I appreciate you letting us do this. Lex is hiding the car around back."

"Not a problem, Ms. Bess. Just glad I could be of help." He poured her a cup of coffee and offered her a seat. "Any luck finding that Wicked Bible?"

"Not yet," she admitted on a sigh. In truth, she'd been more worried about finding Harold Yeager than the Bible, but she supposed she'd have more time to do that once they'd safely transported Harold to jail. Lex had called Brian this morning and given him Yeager's address, and he assured her that Payne would make certain that any copies of her hard drive were destroyed so that Yeager couldn't simply post bail and then go back to work tracing the Bible.

"Shame," Vernon remarked. "I bet whoever has it can put that money to good use."

"I'm sure," she agreed. A moment later, Lex knocked on the door and poked his head inside. Vernon gestured for him to come in, as well—Honey with him, as usual—and handed him a cup of coffee. "Cream and sugar are on the table, young man. Feel free to help yourself."

"Thank you, sir," Lex said.

"That's a fine animal you've got there," Vernon remarked. "Loyal, isn't she?"

Lex grinned. "Very much so."

"I had a dog when I came back from WWII," Vernon said, looking reflective. "I wasn't fit for human company, but my Jack got me through it. He was a German shepherd. Beautiful animal." He jerked his head toward the rear of the house. "He's buried back there. I had him for fifteen years before the cancer got him."

"I'm sorry," Lex said, looking a bit odd. Thoughtful, even.

"You were in the service?" Vernon asked.

Lex grinned. "That obvious, is it?"

"A soldier always recognizes another soldier," he said with a smile. "You see action?"

"I did," Lex admitted. "Took four hits to the shoulder. Messed me up pretty good."

Vernon nodded. "You medic out?"

"It was that or drive a desk all day," Lex told him.

Bess was finding this conversation utterly fascinating. She hadn't been able to get Lex to say a word about his military career and yet Vernon didn't seem to have a problem posing the questions or getting him to answer. Probably because he'd been in the military, as well. Probably because Vernon understood things about that experience that Bess would never be able to.

Vernon grimaced. "Who wants to drive a desk for Uncle Sam? You can do that at home and see your family, not risk your life," he added, chuckling. He paused. "Four rounds into the shoulder, eh? Hit any arteries?"

Lex nodded, carefully swallowing another sip of coffee.

Vernon winced. "A close call then," he said, then gestured toward Honey. "No wonder she's so protective of you. Animals have a sense about stuff like that, you know? My Jack certainly did."

You came close, didn't you? Elsie had said. Bess inwardly gasped and her gaze darted to Lex, who was carefully avoiding looking at her. Four hits to the shoulder? An artery? She saved me? My God, Bess thought. He'd nearly died. Her heart kicked into overdrive and gave a panicked squeeze when she considered what had almost happened to him. When she considered that she'd almost never met him, that he would have never come into her life.

She was breathing too hard, Bess realized, feeling close to hyperventilating. Abruptly she stood and excused herself to the bathroom.

Lex did look at her then, his intriguing blue eyes concerned.

"My biscuit didn't agree with me," she lied, then hurried out of the room. She felt physically ill, ready to vomit, and her hands wouldn't stop shaking. She stared at her chalky reflection for a moment, then splashed water on her face in an effort to try and keep the tears at bay. Tears? For someone she'd known a day? Someone who wasn't even supposed to be that important to her?

He'd nearly died.

And she was already so invested in him—in his life—that she was falling apart.

Lord help her.

11

VERNON WATCHED BESS DART OUT of the room and winced. He sent Lex an apologetic look. "Poor thing. She gets a mite squirrely when you start talking about dying."

"Oh?" Lex remarked, intrigued by her reaction. He hadn't exactly liked talking about his near-death experience in front of her—hadn't talked to anyone much about it at all—but Vernon's matter-of-fact approach had somehow made it easier to share. Probably because the old man was a vet himself and had been through a similar experience. It would have felt disrespectful not to answer his questions.

Furthermore, Vernon's story about Jack, his faithful German shepherd, had given him the purpose he'd been looking for. One moment he'd been sitting here enjoying a good cup of coffee, the next he'd seen his new direction roll out in front of him, one that would allow him to keep his job with Ranger Security, but still be doing something else worthwhile. If Honey had been good for him as a wounded returning soldier and old Jack had been good for Vernon, then there had to be animals that would fill that same purpose for other veterans. Animals that were desperately in need of homes, soldiers who were desperately in need of unconditional love. It was the perfect solution, a beautiful idea, and he was utterly psyched and energized it.

"Yeah," the old man said, looking thoughtful. "I've known her grandfather for a long time, and that little girl has seen more tragedy in her life than what a body ought to have to bear."

Lex leaned forward and winced, silently encouraging Vernon to go on.

"Her daddy was killed in a car wreck when she was seven," the old man said. "That was her granddaddy's boy, mind. Her mother, evidently overcome with grief, committed suicide a year to the day later." He winced. "Terrible stuff."

Lex inwardly swore. No wonder she was "squirrelly about death" as Vernon had so delicately put it. Losing both parents—one to an accident, one deliberate—by the time she was eight.

"Her granddaddy used to bring her over here," he said. "Little slip of a thing, those big eyes in that small face. She didn't talk for about a year after her momma's death, but with some coaxing she finally come along." He smiled. "And she's grown into a lovely girl. Has a good heart, that one. A heart for the world and everything in it. She sees the good in everything, the value in everything. Nothing is worthless to her." Vernon suddenly grinned. "Even a washed-up old creakin'-bones soldier like me."

At that exact moment, Bess walked back into the room. She'd pushed her hair away from her face, but the ends were wet, presumably where she'd splashed water to combat nausea. He knew what that was like, Lex thought.

"You okay?" he asked, wanting to stand up and put his arms around her. But somehow he didn't think she'd appreciate it at the moment. Not in front of Vernon at any rate.

She nodded. "Just got a little sick to my stomach," she said, her smile wobbly and too bright. "I'm fine now."

"That's good," Vernon said, his ears perking up. "Because unless I'm mistaken, that's a Firebird rumbling down my drive."

All senses suddenly on point, Lex stood and moved to the kitchen window. "That's him," he said, adrenaline pumping instantly into his system.

"You got a plan, young man?" Vernon wanted to know.

He nodded. "You just get him through that door,"

Lex told him. "And I'll take care of the rest." He looked to Bess. "You stay where you are. I want him looking at you. That way I'll have the element of surprise."

She nodded, her lips curling slightly. "So I'm bait?"

He chewed the inside of his cheek. "Something like that, yes."

She merely shrugged and settled more firmly against her chair. Thankfully the table was between her and the door, so there was a bit of protection there. Lex heard the engine die and quietly moved behind the door. Every nerve ending was stretched tight with tension. He rested on the balls of his feet, ready for action.

A knock at the door, then Vernon ambled over. "Yes? Can I help you?"

"Good morning, sir. My name is John Smith and I'm a friend of Bess Cantrell's from Bygone's Antiques over in Marietta, Georgia."

From his vantage point behind the door, Lex watched Bess's jaw grow tight as she ground her teeth together.

"Yes, sir, I know Bess," Vernon told him, playing his part to perfection. "How is she doing?"

"She's fine, sir. Just fine. I'm working with her now and am canvassing some of her clients for old books. She's expanding into the rare book market and I wondered if you had anything that would fit that description."

He would have been convincing if most of Bess's clients didn't know her so well. But these were relationships forged by her grandfather and then later built upon by Bess. Most of the people she visited for their "rusty treasure" had watched her grow up. Mr. Yeager here was just too stupid to know it.

Vernon pretended to be thoughtful for a moment. "You know, young man, I think I do have some old books stored back in my spare bedroom." He opened the door wider. "You come on in and take a look at what I've got, since Bess sent you."

Three seconds later, the opportunity presented itself. Yeager stepped deep enough into the kitchen for Lex to strike. One well-placed blow sent the man tumbling to the floor, and before he could struggle or retaliate, Lex had his knee in the small of his back and his arms twisted behind him and cuffed.

"What the hell—"

Lex hauled him to his feet and Bess walked over and stared at him. "Do you know who I am?" she asked.

"Am I supposed to?"

"Bess Cantrell," she said. "And you are no associate of mine." Then to Lex's surprise, she drew her fist back and planted a solid blow directly into Yeager's soft gut. "That was for Stanley Lawson," she said. Her gaze met Lex's. "I can't abide a bully."

Honey growled at Yeager, baring her teeth, and Yeager attempted to kick out and land a blow against the dog. White-hot anger bolted through Lex and he jerked Yeager's arms up. The action wrenched his own shoulder, making him wince with pain. "Watch yourself," he said. "You're already in enough trouble."

Vernon opened the door again and Lex frogmarched their prisoner to the car.

"What are we going to do with him?" Bess asked. "We can't put him in the backseat with Honey."

Lex opened the hatch, then tumbled their prisoner into the back. Before Yeager could orient himself, Lex pulled a big nylon zip tie from his back pocket and secured it tightly around the man's ankles.

"Hey, that hurts!" Yeager yelped. "You can't leave me back here. Kidnappers! Kidnappers!"

Lex unrolled a long strip of duct tape and tore the end with dramatic flourish before slapping it hard over their prisoner's mouth.

Bess grinned, then leaned over. "Strictly speaking," she asked as aside, "is this legal?"

"It's a citizen's arrest," Lex said. "So in the loosest interpretation of the law, yes."

She nodded, seemingly good with that.

They double-checked the cargo area to make sure

there was nothing there that he could use to free himself, then patted him down and removed his keys and wallet and cell phone.

Lex eyed the cell phone and made a mental note to go through it to make sure they weren't missing anything important. He did a quick sweep of the car and found a laptop computer and printout of Bess's client list with little lines drawn through the names of the people he'd already seen. Interestingly enough, he'd divided the map into two sections, the north and the south.

"Bess, you haven't had any calls from clients north of the city, right?"

She looked at the map, a furrow etched between her brows. "No," she said. "Every call has been along his path here."

"My spidey sense is tingling," he said, staring at the map.

"You think he might not have been working alone?"

"I don't know. Every indication is no, but this map…" He shrugged. "It does make me wonder. Why divide it into two sections?"

"If you ask him he's just going to lie," Bess said.

"True. But I've got his cell, and if he's working with someone, then you can bet they'll try to contact him." He looked over at her. "We'll just wait and see if it rings."

"You kicked ass in there," she said, shooting him an admiring look. And, belatedly, it occurred to him that he *had,* that he'd done what he needed to do. A little of the tension he'd been carrying around in his chest lessened.

She reached up on tiptoes and pressed a lingering kiss against his lips. "It was hot," she murmured.

Suddenly so was he. And they had one more night to burn the sheets up.

Once they dropped Yeager off at the jail, the rest of the evening was theirs.

WITH YEAGER STOWED SAFELY in the back, Bess went over and gave Vernon a hug. "Vernon, thanks so much. We couldn't have done this without you."

Smelling like coffee and Old Spice, Vernon returned her embrace. "You're welcome, Bess. You don't be a stranger, you hear? You get on down to see me more often."

"I will," she assured him. "I haven't had a chance to pick lately. We've been too busy chasing after that asshole."

Vernon nodded toward Lex, who was giving Honey a quick turn around the yard before getting back onto the road. "I like your young man. He's a good one."

"He's not my—"

Vernon's shrewd gaze stopped her short. "I haven't

lived as long as I've lived without picking up on a few things," he said. "And I can spot a young couple making moony faces at one another from a hundred yards."

She chuckled. "Moony faces?"

"You know what I mean," he said. "That boy has been through hell. He deserves a little heaven like you. You're good for one another."

"Vernon—"

"Everybody dies, Bess," he said softly. "Hell, I'm at the jumpin'-off place myself."

She gasped and felt her heart squeeze. "Oh, Vernon, you know you've got years ahead of you."

He merely shrugged. "Maybe, maybe not. But I'm ready when my time comes, and whether people are ready or not, it still does. Death is a part of life, Bess, and you can't spend your life avoiding the good things for fear of the bad."

"I'm not—"

He looked at her again. "I'm old, but I'm not blind. Your grandfather used to worry about you, you know. Was worried what would happen to you when he passed. He said that he was afraid that he'd taught you too much about looking in the past for you to want to see any value in the future."

She swallowed and felt tears burn the backs of her lids. He'd said the same thing to her, only a few days before he'd died. A guy had come into the store—a

thirty-something professional with a nice smile—
and had asked her out. She'd said no without really
even considering it. Her grandfather had gotten onto
her then, had told her that she'd better get her head
into her future because she was going to get damned
lonely with only her things.

"Just think about it," Vernon said. He nodded
toward Lex. "That boy is half in love with you already. You give it a little more time and I think they'll
be some wedding bells in your future. The pitter-
patter of little feet, even."

Her chest swelled with some unnamed emotion,
then twisted with bitter regret. That was just it—they
didn't have the time and weren't going to make it.

"We barely know each other," Bess argued.

"Doesn't matter," Vernon told her. "I saw my
Mattie from across the room at a USO dance, then
leaned over and told my buddy I'd just seen the
woman I was going to marry."

She grinned, surprised. "I didn't know that's how
you met Mattie." His sweet wife had lost her battle
with cancer last year.

"She was a nurse," he said. "And she was the most
beautiful woman I'd ever seen. I proposed to her
during our first dance and she blushed and pshawed."
He grinned at her. "A month later she was mine."

"A month?"

"Time was something we didn't want to waste

back then," he said. "That's the mistake you young'uns make now. You take it all for granted."

No doubt he was right, Bess thought, looking at Lex. He had bent down and was rubbing Honey's face, a smile on his own. He wore a dark brown sweater and jeans and the color looked good on him. It made his blue eyes bluer, his hair darker. The jeans were worn and slightly loose, but clung to his ass in a way that made her pulse move more swiftly and her mouth parch.

They had one night left together, one evening in which she could try to slake her lust, to get him out of her system, to let him go.

She reached over and touched her old friend's arm. "Thanks for sharing all of that with me, Vernon. I think I needed to hear it."

"Any time, Bess," he said.

She waved a goodbye, then went and climbed into the passenger seat. The minute she got into the car, Yeager started grunting beneath the duct tape. She thought she recognized the word *bathroom* and merely rolled her eyes, having no sympathy for him whatsoever.

"It's only four hours back to Marietta," she said. "You can hold it."

A pause, then another frantic noise that made her smile.

Lex opened the back door and Honey jumped in.

She peered over the backseat at their trussed-up prisoner, then looked at Lex as if to say, "Really? This is what we're doing?"

Lex just grinned, then slid into the driver's seat. He jerked his head toward the back. "What's his problem?"

"I think he needs to go to the bathroom."

"Too bad," Lex announced in carrying tones, then started the car and, with a wave at Vernon, motored out of the drive.

"What are we going to do about his car?" Bess asked.

"I've left the keys with Vernon, and after he takes it for a joyride, he's going to drop it off at the local police station where they'll impound it."

The whining from the back increased at this news.

Bess grinned. "That's going to get old quick," she said.

"I'll hurry," Lex told her. He picked up his cell and placed a call to Brian. "We've got him," he said by way of greeting. "On our way back now. Right. Yes, she's pleased." He shot Bess a look. "You never mentioned she had such a mean right hook," Lex told him. "Yes, she nailed him, sucker punched him, and he folded like a deck of cards. Seriously." He held the phone away from his mouth. "Payne wants to know if you want a job?"

She chuckled. "Tell him I'm happy with the one I have, thanks."

He relayed her message and brought his boss completely up to speed. "I've got his cell phone and his maps. I'm not altogether certain that he was working alone. I'm going to do a little poking around once we've turned him over to the Marietta PD."

Poking? She sniggered and sent him a look.

Evidently realizing his Freudian slip, he passed a hand over his face to wipe away his smile. Good grief, how was she going to let him go when this was over? Bess thought, melting inside. Why had she ever thought she could? Was Vernon right? Had her grandfather been right? Was she so wrapped up in picking through the past that she was avoiding her future?

All because she was afraid of losing someone?

Vernon had said dying was merely a by-product of living. She supposed so, but she didn't have to like it. Death hadn't been kind to her. It had taken everyone she'd ever cared about and had almost claimed Lex, as well, a man that she'd known had the potential to be special from the first instant she'd seen him. And it hadn't just been the phenomenal sexual attraction.

She'd felt her world move when she'd looked at him, felt the shift in her own heart right from the very beginning.

But could she do it? Could she ask him for more

when she'd already told him that she didn't expect it? Was it fair to change the rules now? To change her mind?

"You've gotten awfully quiet," Lex remarked, shooting her a glance.

She grinned. "You don't have to look so scared."

"Who said I was scared?"

"No one," she said, her lips twisting with humor. "It was the whites of your eyes that gave you away."

He laughed. "You have the strangest sense of humor. But I like it."

She felt the compliment take root and grow. "Thanks. Yours isn't half-bad, either."

"Careful," he warned her. "I might get a big head if you keep showering me with praise like that. Half-bad? Man, that's something right there. Talk about damning with faint praise."

"I didn't realize your ego needed that much stroking," she said. "But now that I do, I'll make more of an effort."

"Who said anything about stroking my ego? If you're going to stroke something, then I'd like to make a suggestion."

She chuckled. "I'll get to that later."

He lowered his voice. "In that tub?"

"You are really interested in my tub, aren't you?"

"Not so much interested in the tub, but the possibilities it presents for…entertainment."

A warm shiver moved through her at the innuendo in his voice. Warmth swirled deep in her womb and settled hotly in her sex and she shifted in her seat. "You need to cut that out," she admonished with a jerk of her head toward the back. "We're not alone."

"But we will be soon enough," he said. He released a shuddering breath. "And I am *so* looking forward to it. Do you know why?" he asked, his voice low and smoky.

She swallowed. "Tell me."

"Because I want to do bad things with you."

12

AT TWO-THIRTY THEY officially handed Harold Yeager and all of his incriminating materials over to the police.

The way Lex had trussed him up like a turkey and hauled him from Dothan in the back of his car provided an endless laugh at Yeager's expense, and when the police had not-very-carefully removed the duct tape from his mouth, he'd cursed until the air turned blue and accused them of inhumane treatment. Evidently he'd guzzled a huge amount of cola before arriving at Vernon's and his bladder had been near explosion for the past four hours.

To which Bess has replied, "Too damned bad."

She'd had absolutely no sympathy for him whatsoever and no one else, Lex included, could blame her.

He loaded Honey into the car, then slid back

behind the driver's seat. He'd taken a big breath
and just finished releasing it when Bess suddenly
launched herself at him, sweet lips impatient, insis-
tent and warm. He'd been fighting visions of their
naked bodies in her tub all the way back from Dothan
and he'd had to struggle to keep everything in focus.

Now the only thing he wanted to focus on was
Bess, and she, thank God, seemed to be of the same
mind. She tore her mouth from his and rained kisses
along his jaw, over his cheeks, and pushed her hands
into his hair. He felt her breasts press against his
chest, all womanly and soft, and her hair slid over the
backs of his hands as he framed her face, desperate
to simply taste her, to simply feel her against him.

She kissed him deeply again, made a deep moan-
ing low in her throat that literally lit him up, and then
drew back and settled into her seat once more.

"There," she said, as though she'd just completed
something important. "Do you feel better?" she
asked, throwing his words right back at him.

He chuckled and shook his head. "Not as good as I
know I'm going to feel in a few minutes." A thought
struck. "What are we going to do about Elsie?"

She frowned. "I'll check in with her and tell her
that I'm tired."

"Will that keep her from coming into the backyard?"

Her lips twitched. "It will keep her from coming

over, yes." She guided him through the back way so that he could park his car where it wouldn't be visible from the store and he listened as Bess once again was subjected to more of Elsie's "feelings."

Since he'd had the same impression regarding this case as Elsie, it hardly seemed fair to scoff at her, so he didn't. They'd scrolled through the numbers on Yeager's phone and, other than discovering he was a mama's boy, hadn't found anything especially suspicious. That hadn't kept Lex from feeling like there was still more going on here, but until any possible accomplice tipped his hand, they had nothing to go on.

Bess had double-checked the northern addresses and had asked Elsie once again if she'd had any strange phone calls. She hadn't. For the time being, they'd done everything they could do…and he just wanted to do her.

Her house was everything he would have expected. Though it didn't appear cluttered in the least, there was still a lot of stuff inside. Knickknacks on the antique mantel, an old brass bucket filled with wood. The walls were painted in soft muted tones, drawing color from her belongings rather than the actual architecture of the house. He noted dark hardwoods and lots of bead board, and the scent of cinnamon and cherry tobacco smoke hung in the air.

Severus, her cat, strolled haughtily into the room,

took one look at Honey and arched his back. With a hiss, he shot out again like a streak of black lightning.

Bess chuckled. "Well, that went well."

"Is he going to be all right?"

"Yeah," she said. "He'll hide for a while, then he'll get curious and come out." She looked up at him. "You don't think Honey would hurt him, do you?"

"No," he said. "She probably couldn't even get close enough to try. Severus is fast."

Bess wrapped her arms around his waist, then lifted her mouth up for a kiss. Desire bolted through him, hot and furious, and suddenly he couldn't wait for the tub, couldn't wait to have her, couldn't stand not feeling her naked flesh beneath his hands, beneath his mouth, around his dick.

She drew back, threaded her fingers through his, then tugged him toward the back porch. "You tend the fire and I'll run the bath," she said.

Evidently he would have to wait, he thought as they stepped outside. She hadn't been lying about her backyard. The privacy fence was taller than the average fence, with lots of evergreens around the perimeter, and she'd also hung long shades at either end of the porch. Could someone see in her backyard? Yes. If they were very determined. But why would anyone go to the trouble unless they knew she was back here?

He tended the fire, as she asked, and listened to the water run into the big tub. When he turned around, the breath literally whooshed out of him. She'd already removed her clothes, tied her hair up and was lying back, letting the warm water sluice over her skin. Steam rose off the water, curling in little swirls around her.

Wet naked skin, pink-capped breasts, a womanly belly, a thatch of dark red curls between her thighs.

It was the exact picture his imagination had shared with him and he went instantly hard. She looked up then and smiled at him, her green eyes darkened with desire, and he felt the world tilt on its axis. His heart gave a squeeze so painful it pushed even more air out of his lungs.

"You coming in?" she asked, her voice low and sultry.

Oh, hell, yeah. With deliberate precision Lex put a condom on the little wrought-iron table next to the tub, then quickly whipped his sweater over his head and shucked his jeans. Her hungry gaze drifted over him and her lashes dropped to half-mast when she saw his erection jutting proudly forward.

"Come here," she said, swallowing.

She wanted him, Lex thought, and didn't disguise it, didn't play coy. She wanted him and wanted to let him know that she did.

He sidled forward and slipped into the tub with

her, sloshing water over the side. Warmth immediately enveloped him, both from her and the bath, and he settled against the back of the tub and drew her to him. She crawled up his body and kissed him, feeding at his mouth, sliding her hands over him with a greedy, desperate touch that almost set him off.

"I've been thinking about doing this out here with you from the moment I saw you," she confided. "I wanted you…instantly. That's shameless of me, isn't it?"

"No," he said, sliding his tongue down her throat, then lifting her up so that he could suckle her breasts, taste her pouting nipples. "Not at all. I didn't know about your little garden of Eden out here. But I wanted you, too. And I thought you knew. I thought you could tell."

She grinned and gasped as he worshipped her with his mouth. Reaching between them, she took him in hand, working the slippery skin against her small palm.

"I could," she said. "And it made me feel all warm and wicked."

He was going to come if she didn't stop talking to him this way, Lex thought. He was going to lose it completely…and that would be a tragedy because he wasn't anywhere near done with her yet.

He slid a finger into her curls and was gratified when she gave a little gasp of pleasure. He loved those sounds she made, those mewling noises of satisfaction. Each one was like a reward, an atta boy for his penis, making it harder. She was warm and slick beneath his fingers and she worked herself against him, her neck going a little boneless as she did so, her eyes drifting shut. And then it wasn't enough. He needed to be inside her, wanted to feel her greedy little body clamping around him when she came.

He grabbed the condom, made quick work of putting it on and then pulled her back on top of him. She bent forward and kissed him again, angling their bodies so his dick nudged her entrance. And then with a blissful sigh of ultimate satisfaction, she slowly lowered herself onto him.

She closed around him completely, took every bit of him she could, from root to tip, and squeezed her pleasure.

"Ahhh," she moaned. "That's better. Now I can breathe."

And he knew exactly what she meant, because he felt the same way. He felt like everything that had been wrong with his world had suddenly been put right. There was something profoundly significant in that thought, and whereas he would have avoided it yesterday, today, on the eve of never seeing her again, he couldn't.

Something about this girl simply spoke to him on a level he didn't understand and probably never would.

Why did some people like chocolate and others vanilla? If you asked those people, they wouldn't know the reason, only the preference.

And that's how he felt about Bess.

He didn't know why he liked her best out of all the girls he'd ever met. He didn't know exactly what it was that made her special, the yin to his yang, the nut for his screw—no pun intended.

She completed him…and Lex knew he'd never be the same without her.

BESS WRAPPED HERSELF as firmly around Lex as she could and savored the feel of him against her. *Soft, sleek skin, smooth muscle over bone, masculine hair abrading her chest, the long hard length of him buried deeply inside of her.*

And that mouth, she thought, the ultimate instrument of her sexual torture. Full and beautiful, carnal and wicked, and the things he did with it.

He flexed beneath her, filling her up completely, and she found his mouth once more, kissing him deeply. She pushed her hands into his hair and aligned their bodies more tightly. He was big and hard and wonderful and she loved the way he made her feel, petite and tiny, protected and safe.

Strange, that last, Bess thought, because she'd never been afraid to live alone, had never minded it at all. She'd always been confident in her ability to protect herself. So what exactly did he make her feel safe from? she wondered, and knew something important lurked in that revelation.

He pushed up again and the thought vanished from her head like ether.

"Do you have any idea how good you feel," he said, his big hands slipping up her back. "Do you know how crazy you make me?"

She laughed. "I've got a pretty good idea," she said. "Because I'm in the same fictional mental hospital, just in a different padded room."

She felt him chuckle against her lips and let the sound melt against her tongue.

"I'll share my padded room with you," he said, flexing up into her again and upping his tempo. "So long as we can continue to do this."

She tightened around him, loving the delicious drag and draw between their joined bodies, the water swirling around them, the steam rising over them. From the corner of her eye she saw Honey lying on the rug near the door and she grinned.

"What's so funny?"

"Honey's out here," she said, chuckling.

"Is she watching us?"

"No."

"Good," he said. "She's a smart dog." He leaned forward and circled her nipple with his hot tongue, then pulled it into his mouth and suckled deeply.

She felt that tug all the way to the heart of her sex as though an invisible thread connected the two, and she gasped at the pleasure arcing through her.

"Ah," he said. "That's better. If you've got time to look at the dog, then clearly I'm not doing this right."

He flexed more deeply into her and she came down as he went up, settling into a mind-numbingly wonderful rhythm.

"Oh, I don't know about that," Bess told him, leaning forward to kiss his mangled shoulder. "I'd say you were doing better than average."

"Average?" He feigned outrage, anchoring his hands on either side of her hips. "Average?" he repeated. "Damn, woman. I would hope you'd expect more of me than that."

She chuckled, felt the first bit of climax quicken in her womb, take root deep in the heart of her sex. Her clit throbbed and she sighed, working herself more firmly against him.

"I'm not worried," she told him. "I'm sure you're going to give m-me your b-best effort."

He smiled up at her and his grin was so wicked she felt it tingle her nipples. "You're playing with me, aren't you? You're purposely trying to drive me insane."

"That's the best way to keep you in that little padded room with me," she told him. "So I can tear your clothes off and do bad things with you."

He laughed again and pounded into her, pushing her higher and higher toward the peak of ecstasy. "There's a better way, you know? An easier way."

She bit her bottom lip and felt her lids droop as the orgasm came nearer and nearer. This wasn't going to be a huge explosion of sensation, Bess realized. It was going to build and build and then erupt slowly and linger. It was going to sap her strength and make her melt and go boneless.

"How's that?" she murmured,

"Just ask."

And with that little comment, he pushed her over the edge and she went free-falling into bliss. She moaned long and low, the sound almost inhuman. Her head suddenly became too heavy for her neck and she sagged forward against him, letting the pleasure wash through her. She tightened around him over and over and the sensation detonated additional little fireworks in her womb. It went on and on and she thought she was going to pass out from the joy of it, from the perfection.

A moment later she felt Lex stiffen beneath her and he pushed harder, deeper and then harder still. He raced toward release and then flung himself over the edge and made the rest of the fall with her. His long growl of masculine satisfaction resonated in her soul, and he cradled her closer, unable to get enough of her. He slid his fingers along her spine, feeling every ridge and bump, and then drew back and kissed her again.

There was something heartbreakingly tender about the gesture and it took her a moment to discern what it was. The desire was there—the desperate all-consuming hammering need. But there was something else, as well. Something tender and special, something she hadn't felt in a long, long time.

Affection.

Tears burned in her eyes and she determinedly blinked them away.

Time was something we didn't want to waste back then, Vernon had said. And she didn't want to waste any more of it, either.

A strange noise reached her ears and she leaned back and looked at Lex.

A frown furrowed his brow, then comprehension dawned and his gaze slammed into hers. "Yeager's phone," he said, scrambling forward.

Bess moved quickly out of the way and, not bothering to grab a towel, hurried after him into the house. She found Lex in the kitchen, completely nude, Yeager's cell phone next to his ear.

"It was his mother again," Lex said. "She's left a voice mail."

She watched his expression go from alert attentiveness to lethal. "She's helping him," he said, swearing hotly. "She's in Alpharetta, on her way to Roswell, and wants to know why he hasn't checked in."

Bess frowned. "Roswell?" Dripping wet, she grabbed her map off the kitchen counter and started comparing it to her client list. Judith Henkins, Bess thought and an image suddenly loomed large in her mind. The counter, the Coca-Cola sign. It had been in her old store next to her house.

Oh, God.

He disconnected. "Bess?"

"I know where it is and she's going to get to it first."

"Oh, hell, no, she isn't," Lex said. "Call your contact now and let them know what's going on. Evidently she's been extremely nice, telling people that she was your grandfather's sister, and no one has asked any questions. She just ridiculed her son's conspicuous approach and told him to call her immediately. I'm going to contact the police and see if I can get them to delay any phone call he might make to her so he can't alert her to the fact that we've got him and are now undoubtedly aware of her. If she feels cornered, who knows what she might do."

Bess nodded and grabbed her phone, then quickly dialed Judith's number and swore when she didn't get an answer.

"Dry off and get dressed," he said. "You can keep

calling her from the car and we'll alert the police over there, as well."

She was so upset she knew she wouldn't have thought of that. Her nerves stretched to the breaking point, Bess made quick work of getting back into her clothes and didn't bother trying to do anything to her hair. Three minutes later they were in the car, Honcy looking mystified, and headed toward Roswell.

"How long does it take to get there?" Lex asked her.

"About twenty minutes if we don't have any traffic issues."

"And from Alpharetta to Roswell?"

She felt sick. "About ten to fifteen."

He muttered a hot oath.

"We're not going to make it in time, are we?" she said, frantically dialing Judith again. "We're going to be too late."

Lex practically stood on the gas, grim determination in every line of his face. "Not if I can help it."

13

EVEN THOUGH HE KNEW THAT it wouldn't have made a difference if they hadn't been at her house having sex, Lex nevertheless felt a bit guilty all the same. Logically, he knew that until that call had come in, they'd had no idea that Yeager's mother had been in on the scheme with him, or that she'd been going around, canvassing the northern part of the state. No one had called because she'd been nice, nonthreatening and polite.

In between frantically dialing Judith, Bess had made a few calls to some of her other clients and they'd all confirmed that an older woman, who'd claimed to be her grandfather's sister, had been coming by. She'd given the same "rare books" spiel as her son, but she'd delivered it with a jar of home-made strawberry preserves and a smile.

Lex hadn't met her—yet, he qualified—but anyone who was capable of canvassing an area with the intent to steal something of value from someone who didn't know its worth was a particularly nasty kind of thief. She wasn't any better than her low-life scum of a son, Lex thought.

Bess growled an angry sound and disconnected her cell phone, then hit Redial again. "I can't get her," she said. "But I have to keep trying."

"We're almost there. Just a few more minutes."

"She's not answering because she's not in the house. The bitch has already gotten there. Oh, Lex. What if we're too late?"

"So long as she's not hurt, it'll be fine, Bess," he reassured her. "We know who the woman is, we can find out where she lives. If we miss her here, we'll make sure to get her at some point between here and her house." In fact, he'd call Payne now. He should have already done that, but was afraid his boss would wonder what they'd been doing with the downtime between dropping Yeager off and now, and he really didn't want to go into it while Bess was in the car.

He would have to at some point, he knew, but... not in front of her.

He dialed Payne and quickly brought him up to speed on the situation. "We're about two minutes out, but Bess can't get Mrs. Henkins on the phone and suspects that it's because Yeager's mother has already arrived and they've gone out to her shop. I've called the local police and alerted them, but would like some Ranger Security backup en route now to Mrs. Yeager's house."

"Done," Payne told him. "Anything else?"

"No, that should get it."

"Update me when you can," he said. "And tell Bess I said we'll make this right no matter what."

Meaning that he'd personally give Mrs. Henkins the value of the book if he botched this. Lex whistled low and had a whole new dimension of respect for his boss. He told Bess what Payne had said and, to his horror, saw her bottom lip tremble.

Oh, God, no. Not tears. Anything but tears. "Hey, hey, hey," he said soothingly, reaching over to put a finger against her lip to quell the quiver. "It's going to be okay. We're going to take care of this. Do you believe me?"

"I want to," she said. "But I'm so afraid that this psychotic woman is going to do something horrible and hurt Mrs. Henkins."

"Bess, she's managed to charm everyone else. She's wily enough to know that you get more flies with honey than you do vinegar."

"I know, but—"

"So she's not going to change her MO now. It's working for her. Mrs. Henkins is going to be fine. I promise you. I have a gut feeling about this."

That cracked a smile. "You and Elsie," she said

with a weak eye roll. "I'm surrounded by amateur psychics."

"I've never claimed to be psychic," he said. "I just try to pay more attention to my instincts. If I'd listened to them in Iraq I wouldn't have taken those hits to the shoulder and nearly died." There. He'd told her. She'd heard it at Vernon's, of course, but that was different. That wasn't him trusting her enough to share it directly.

"You don't have to tell me anything, Lex," she said. "I know you don't want to talk about it."

"It's not easy," he admitted. "I thought for sure that I was going to die, was completely convinced that my life was over." He swallowed. "And you want to know the terrible part? When they told me I could medic out, that I could leave, I was *happy*. I was relieved." He swallowed. "Because nearly dying had made me a coward."

She whirled on him, her eyes rounding with outrage. "A coward? Are you insane? Nearly dying didn't make you a coward! It made you appreciate life enough to want to take yourself out of the line of fire! It made you want to live! That's not cowardly, you fool. That's called self-preservation."

He wished he could look at it that way, Lex thought skeptically. It would be so much easier to live with what had happened.

"Let me ask you something, Lex. How long were

you in the military? How many years? How many
tours of duty?"

"I spent four years in ROTC, then eight years in
active service. Four tours of duty in that time."

"Because we've been at war. Because your country needed you. Did you ever at any time turn around
and run from your enemy? Did you hide and watch
other people die to save yourself?"

He recoiled, horrified. "No," he said. "Of course
not."

"Do you know why?" she asked. "You know
why you didn't do those things? Because you're not
a coward, because you are a man of honor who fought
for his country and sacrificed a part of himself for
it." She shook her head and a tear slipped down one
cheek. "Don't ever call yourself a coward again, because that's not who you are at all." She was quiet for
a moment. "You know who was a coward? A selfish
coward?" she asked him, and he knew what she was
going to say, thanks to Vernon.

"My mother," she said. "I told you that my parents were dead, but I didn't tell you what happened."
She released a small breath. "My father died in a
car accident when I was seven. A year later, to the
day, my mother put a bullet through her brain. Because she was too afraid of living on her own and
too wrapped up in her own grief to care about me.
She was a coward, a weak selfish one who was sick,

I know, but it still applies. *She* was a coward. You, on the other hand, simply wanted to live." She smiled sadly. "And there's no shame in that."

The pain in her voice, the sadness in her eyes would have brought him to his knees had he been standing. No wonder she didn't let herself get attached to people, Lex thought. Because people, even her grandfather when he'd died, always let her down. That's why no one had ever snapped her up. That's why she hadn't married. That's why she'd put him off with her I-don't-have-any-expectations speech.

Because she didn't.

And she never let herself hope that anyone was going to be different—even him—because in her life it had never happened.

He didn't know when he'd felt this helpless. He didn't know how to comfort her. Didn't know how to make it right for her.

But he wished he did.

"Turn here," she said, gesturing to a long rutted driveway on his left. She peered ahead. "The white car is Judith's. The blue one I don't recognize, so it's probably Yeager's mother."

Anticipation spiked as he pulled in behind the blue car, deliberately blocking it so the driver would have a hard time pulling out.

"Are you armed?" she said.

He nodded. To his shock, so was she. She pulled

a pistol from her purse and slipped it beneath the waistband of her jeans. "Bess, where did you get that? You—"

"I know what I'm doing, Lex," she said, and there was a cool assurance in her voice that told him it was the truth.

He shook his head. Was there anything this woman couldn't do?

"Let's go," she said. "I'm sure they're in the shop."

Determined to do some part of his job correctly, Lex took point and put himself between Bess and the shop. Honey, of course, did the same thing for him. He really should have left her in the car, but didn't have the heart. She could sense his tension and had been nosing his elbow the entire way here.

"Mrs. Henkins?" Lex called as he walked carefully into her shop.

"Yes," the older woman called.

Bess came around him, ducking beneath his arm. "Judith, I've been trying to call."

Judith looked momentarily confused. "Bess?"

The woman with her—Mrs. Yeager—whirled around and smoothly pulled a gun from her purse. "Well, well," she said. "You couldn't leave well enough alone, could you? You just had to interfere."

Seeing the gun in Mrs. Yeager's hand, Judith gasped. "Mrs. Ogletree! Put that gun away at once!"

"I wouldn't have had to draw it at all if they hadn't

shown up." She glanced at Bess. "Now someone is going to get hurt and it's going to be all your fault."

BESS'S HEART DROPPED to her feet and, for one terrifying moment, she thought she might faint. Then Lex found her icy fingers and gave them a squeeze and the comfort from that one gesture restored her in a way she would have never believed. A peace came over her like a long shimmering veil.

"I've got this," he whispered, and she knew it was true. She knew in that instant that everything was going to be fine.

"Mrs. Henkins, my name is Lex Sanborn and I'm with Ranger Security. My firm was hired by Bess after someone broke into her shop and stole the external hard drive from her computer."

"It doesn't matter why you're here," Mrs. Yeager sneered. She held up the book and wagged it significantly. "I've already got it. It's too late. She's going to sell it to me."

"I never said that—" Judith protested.

Mrs. Yeager whirled on her and wagged the gun in her face. "Whether you sell it to me or not, I'm taking it."

"No, you are not," Bess told her. "Your son is already in jail and the police are en route here now. In the event that you manage to evade them, then Ranger Security—who don't operate with the same set of rules as regular law enforcement—will follow you to the ends of the earth. You will *never* be able to sell that book and you'll *never* see a penny of the money."

Judith frowned. "Money? What money?" she asked. "It's just an old Bible."

Mrs. Yeager cackled madly. "See?" she said. "She doesn't deserve the money! She doesn't even know what it's worth!"

"But it's still hers," Lex pointed out. "Now put the gun away and set the book down. I really don't want to hurt you." But the lead in his voice said he would if he had to.

Evidently smart enough to take him seriously, but not intelligent enough to do what he said, Mrs. Yeager turned and aimed the gun right at Judith's head.

Bess gasped and her friend's face went white with fear.

"You move over against the back wall," Mrs. Yeager told Judith, indicating the space farthermost from the door. "And you go with her," she said to Lex. She looked at Bess. "You're coming with me."

Bess frowned. "What?"

She gestured angrily with the gun. "You're coming with me," she repeated angrily, then sneered at Lex. "Insurance to keep him from doing anything stupid."

Honey growled and crouched low.

"No, Honey," Lex told the dog, and, though it was clear he didn't want to follow the woman's order, it was also clear that he didn't see an alternative. Reluctantly, he and Bess did as she said, Honey growling all the while. The hair was standing up on the back of her neck and Bess knew the only thing that was keeping the dog from attacking Mrs. Yeager was Lex's command.

"That's it," Mrs, Yeager said. "Do what I say and no one will get hurt."

With the gun still firmly aimed at Bess, she started inching toward the door. "Come on," she said. "In the event he tries to be a hero, I want you between me and him."

"I don't understand," Judith called desperately. "Why do you want that book so badly?"

"Because it's a Wicked Bible, you old fool! Ever heard of it?"

Judith shook her head. "No."

"It's also called the Adulterous Bible and the Sinner's Bible." Seemingly unable to resist showing her superiority, Mrs. Yeager carefully opened the book to the right place and held it up for Bess to see. "Look there," she said. "Read it. Exodus 20:14."

Bess did, not seeing a choice.

Judith gasped. "That's not right," she said. "It's a mistake."

Mrs. Yeager smiled malevolently. "That's a hundred-thousand-dollar mistake," she said. "And I am very much looking forward to cashing in on it."

If possible, Judith paled even more. "A hundred thousand dollars? You're telling me that old Bible is worth a hundred thousand dollars?"

"I am," she said, then dragging Bess with her, turned and darted out the door with more speed and agility than Bess would have imagined, given her age.

Once they were outside, Mrs. Yeager turned and shoved Bess to the ground, then ran. Bess immediately bolted up and gave chase. She could hear Lex behind her, gaining ground.

Bess withdrew her gun and trained it on Mrs. Yeager's retreating back. "Stop or I'll shoot!" Bess yelled.

Mrs. Yeager turned and, upon seeing the gun, fired a shot in Bess's direction. Time slowed to a crawl and suddenly everything went into slow motion. Mrs. Yeager's eyes widened with anger and, seemingly incensed that Bess would point a gun at her, fired again. The shot rang out, and with a furious shout, Lex jumped in front of her, shoving her to safety. At the same time, Honey leaped in front of Lex.

"Honey!" Lex bellowed as the dog yelped.

"I'll take care of her," Bess told him. "Get that bitch!"

Lex put on a burst of speed and tackled the old

woman to the ground before she could get to her car. Another shot rang out, scaring more years off Bess's life, but there was no gasp of pain. Seconds later, Lex had wrenched the weapon away from Yeager's mother and jerked her to her feet.

The police pulled in then, lights flashing, sirens blaring, and took control of the situation. Seemingly satisfied that everything was under control, Lex hurried over to Bess and gathered Honey into his arms.

"She jumped up," he said, his voice breaking. "She jumped right in front of me. I told her to stay down, but she just—"

Bess inspected the wound, which was bleeding profusely. "It's her ear, Lex," she said. "That's all. Yeager barely nicked her, but—"

"There's so much blood. How can there be so much blood?"

She took his face in her hands. "Lex, it's just the nature of the wound. They bleed a lot. Trust me, she's going to be fine. Truly."

Her words seemed to sink in and he breathed a deep sigh of relief. The terror on his face when he thought he'd lost his dog was almost more than she could bear.

"What did you think she'd do if she figured you were in danger?" she asked him, petting the dog gently. "Stand by and watch you get hurt?" She grinned. "You know that's not Honey's style."

He managed a weak chuckle.

"And what about you? You jumped in front of me. I didn't get to be anyone's hero today." She knew that it was his job, that protecting her was something he was supposed to do, but she didn't think she'd ever been more touched by anything. He'd been willing to die for her, willing to give his life to keep her safe.

And the fool was afraid he was a coward.

A blinking look of comprehension slowly settled on his face. "I did, didn't I?"

Tears leaking from her eyes, Bess nodded. "You did."

Hours later, after Mrs. Yeager had been hauled away to jail, Judith had been inspected by a paramedic—she'd fallen trying to run out of the shop—and deemed fine, and Honey's ear had been stitched up by the local vet, Lex pulled into her driveway and turned to face her.

She knew without asking that he wasn't going to stay, that he was going to take his dog home and finish his report on his first assignment.

She knew…and yet she wasn't prepared.

A lump filled in her throat and she twisted her fingers in her hands. "Thank you," she said, though it seemed horribly inadequate. "You don't know how much I've appreciated—and enjoyed—the past couple of days with you."

He studied her for a minute, his eyes rife with

hidden meaning. Regret? Yes. But there was something more, something she couldn't quite put her finger on.

"Listen, Bess—"

She didn't know what he was going to say, but couldn't let him finish. She'd rather believe that he was going to tell her that things didn't have to end this way, that they could give it a go and see where this took them. She'd rather convince herself of that than let him say the exact opposite.

Was she in love with him? Was this what love felt like? She honestly didn't know. But she knew when he pulled out of her driveway, when he and his sweet dog ultimately drove away, he'd be taking a little piece of her with him, a little bit of hope that she'd managed to latch on to.

"I'd better get inside," she said. She opened the car door and slipped out. Hesitated before closing it.

"Bess," he said, regret making his voice deeper, more compelling.

"Bess!" Elsie called, and for once Bess was grateful for her interference.

Lex sighed and nodded, then slowly drove away.

Elsie took one look at her face and wrapped her in a warm hug. She tsked against her hair. "I told you that you were in danger," the older woman said.

"Yes, but you didn't say which part," Bess sniffled.

14

LEX HAD TOLD HIMSELF that distance was the cure for what ailed him. That if he simply busied himself with enough work, enough effort, he'd eventually come to see that his whirlwind romance with Bess hadn't been as spectacular as he imagined. That he'd been too long without a woman, that the attraction between them was a hyped-up figment of his imagination.

He kept telling himself this, but could never quite bring himself to believe it.

When he looked around his apartment now, it felt cold and unlived in. In fact, the only parts that didn't feel that way were the things he was certain Payne had bought from Bess. There was an old photo of a lone wolf above his mantel, the animal trudging through the snow, looking longingly over his shoulder. For what? the picture made one wonder. Had the wolf heard something and turned around? Or was he leaving something behind, but wished he wasn't?

A big antique jug with a cork top sat in the foyer and a quick look on eBay confirmed it was early Georgian pottery. An old colander rested a top of his kitchen cabinets along with various bottles of unknown origin, but they were pretty and had character all the same.

Lex was certain those, too, had come from Bess.

On a brighter note, Payne had been very complimentary about how he'd handled the case, and though he was certain Bess hadn't said a word, when he looked at Payne he knew his boss was aware that something had happened between them. He didn't ask, though, and as of yet, Lex hadn't been able to summon the nerve to tell him.

As soon as he found time, Lex had gone to the local animal shelter and his local VA and made arrangements to try and place dogs with veterans— both young and old. In only a week he'd successfully found two animals a home. Though he knew there were good dogs in the no-kill shelters as well, right now he was only working with the county animal control because those dogs were the ones at risk.

For the first time in his life he felt like he was truly making the kind of difference that spoke to his soul, and he wished that he could share the experience with Bess, wished that he could tell her how wonderful saving both the animals and their new owners felt. It was beyond fabulous to see the joy, the instant devotion on both sides.

When he'd said that Honey had saved him, he hadn't realized how true that was until now.

A knock sounded at his door and he shot Honey a look—she ordinarily barked—then went to answer it. Bess? he wondered. Was she regretting their no-strings arrangement as much as he was?

Lex opened the door and blinked in shock. "Elsie?"

Elsie lifted her chin. "May I come in or are you going to leave me standing out in the hall like a fool?"

He blinked. "No, of course not," he said. "Come on in. Can I get you something to drink? A soda, tea, beer?"

She nodded to the Scotch on the counter, the bottle he'd yet to open. "I'll have some of that," she said. "Two fingers and don't be stingy with it. It's rude."

He fond it especially ironic that she was the one lecturing him on what was rude. Baffled, he did as she asked and handed her the glass.

Dressed like a geriatric call girl in black leggings and a leopard-print shirt, she plopped herself down in his recliner and took a grateful sip.

"So," she said. "What's the problem?"

He frowned, not following. "I'm sorry?"

She chuckled. "Oh, you're going to be if you don't fix this."

"Fix what?"

"My girl's heart," she said. "What are you doing toying with her affections like that, then taking off for parts unknown?"

In the first place he hadn't realized he'd toyed with Bess's affections—he thought he was doing what she wanted. And in the second place, she could hardly accuse him of taking off to parts unknown when she'd managed to show up at his apartment. "I'm sorry, Elsie," he said. "But I really don't think this is any of your business."

"You think I don't know that, fool! I don't care if it's my business or not. You are *ruining* my reputation."

"What?"

"As a psychic," she went on, as though he were the slow one. "I've told everyone—with the exception of Bess, of course—that I saw the love of her life walk in the door and that she was going to be blissfully happy." She glared at him. "You were supposed to do that. You were supposed to make her blissfully happy, and instead, you've made her miserable." She looked down at his feet. "Now get your shoes on and go fix it."

Lex was so confused he didn't even know where to start. If he was understanding this incomprehensible mess correctly, Elsie had had a vision of him and Bess being "blissfully happy" together, and now, because he'd made Bess miserable, Elsie was losing face with her friends.

Ultimately none of that mattered except for the "Bess was miserable" part.

That was intolerable.

But why was she miserable? She was the one who'd said that she didn't have any expectations. She'd even indicated that she'd be happier without them.

After a moment, he said as much to Elsie. "Look, Elsie, Bess didn't want this relationship to go any further than it did. She said—"

"I don't give a damn what she said. She's scared. She doesn't want to get hurt. She's always afraid that she's going to love someone and they're going to leave her, either willingly like her mother, or accidentally like her father and grandfather. But I've known her since she was a little girl, and I'm telling you, she's never felt this way about a man before. She's never pined the way she's pining for you."

"But—"

"Do you want her?" Elsie asked.

More than his next breath. He nodded. "I think she's the most amazing woman in the entire world," he said simply.

"Then go to her, Lex." She smiled sadly. "If

anyone ever deserved a happily ever after, it's my Bess. And what about you? What about appreciating life now that you've got a second chance? Or was that just hogwash?"

He stilled and slid her a look. He'd never said anything like that to her. He hadn't been around her enough. And he hadn't said it to Bess, either.

Elsie merely smiled. "I keep my telepathic talents to myself," she said. "Freaks people out when they discover you can read their minds."

And with that enigmatic comment, she stood.

"And for the record, this is not a leopard-print shirt—it's a tiger—and I do *not* look like a geriatric call girl."

She harrumphed and made her way to the door. "Go to her. Now. She's at the shop, working in the back, trying to find something in all that mess that can plug the hole in her heart. And you're the only thing that's going to do it."

Lex stilled, absorbing everything that Elsie had just told him, then leaped into action. He freshened up, put on his shoes, then clipped the leash onto Honey's collar and made his way downstairs.

"Where are you going in such a hurry?" Flanagan asked.

"To see Bess."

"'Bout time," Flanagan muttered with a grin.

Lex shot him a questioning look over his shoulder.

"Elsie's good friends with Payne," he explained. "Forget having any secrets around here."

Lex laughed and shook his head, then pushed his way outside.

The only secret he had right now was the one he'd kept from Bess…and he was about to share it with her.

"DAMMIT," BESS MUTTERED as she heard the bell tinkle above the door. She heaved herself up from the floor and dusted her bottom off. Elsie had said something about needing a few hours off, so Bess was minding the store instead of working on the elaborate inventory of the back room that she'd started a week ago.

And what had brought about this sudden, manic urge to catalog every item in her store?

The absence of a really tall, really special, wicked-mouthed man.

She was a mess, Bess thought. A miserable, wretched, stupid mess.

"Be right there," she called. She checked her reflection to make sure that she didn't have any dirt on her face, then made her way to the front of the store. She saw the back of his head first, then his profile—his woefully familiar profile. Her heart gave a lurch and her step faltered.

"Lex?" What was he doing here? she wondered. How in the hell was she supposed to get over him if he was going to arbitrarily show up here anytime he wanted?

His beautiful blue gaze slammed into hers and she felt the earth move, the ground shake, her very foundation crumble. He smiled at her with that wicked mouth and lust pure and unadulterated speared through her, making her mouth go dry and her eyes dampen.

Shit. She didn't want to cry.

"Bess," he said, coming forward. His gaze raked over her frame, stealing along her curves, resting briefly on her breasts, then fastened on her eyes. The heat and longing in his were unmistakable, and for a moment she wondered if he'd been as acutely miserable as she had. If he'd known half the agony she'd been in.

Agony of her own making—it had been her rules after all—but misery all the same.

She just wanted him. Desperately. With every fiber of her being, down to her very core. And if this wasn't love, then it would be soon enough, and she wanted that, too, wanted to feel every bit of emotion, savor all the ups and downs. She wanted to go to sleep with him at night and wake up with him in the morning. She wanted to bathe with him on her back porch and roast marshmallows in her chiminea. She wanted to take care of him when he was sick, and work puzzles with him and walk on the beach and explore the mountains and…everything.

She couldn't think of a single thing that wouldn't be made better by his presence in her life.

She just wanted him. And hoped that his being here meant he wanted her, too.

"What are you doing here?" she asked faintly. "Is something wrong?"

"The only thing that's wrong with me is that I haven't seen you," he said. "Look, Bess, I know that you said you didn't have any expectations, but…I do."

Her heart gave a squeeze and pleasure bloomed in her chest. "You do?"

"Yes," he said. "I expected you to give us a chance. I expected you to call me. I expected you to tell me that you'd made a mistake, that you wanted to give this a go and see where it would lead. I expected you to tell me that you didn't know what might happen between us, but that you were intrigued enough and cared enough about me to want to try. I expected—"

"I'm sorry, Lex," she said, swallowing tightly. "I was scared. I was so afraid of something going wrong, of getting hurt, that I couldn't bring myself to take a chance." She paused. "*I* was a coward."

He took a step forward and his eyes were kind and soft with affection. She soaked it in, wanted to bathe in it, "That's not being a coward, Bess—that's called self-preservation," he corrected, throwing her words back at her. "But I can promise you this. I would never, ever intentionally hurt you, I don't think I could."

She launched herself at him, wrapping her arms around him. Tears streamed down her cheeks as she kissed his neck, his face, his eyelids and then his mouth—oh, his mouth, how she'd missed it. She savored the feel of him against her lips, his taste on her tongue.

"I have a secret," he said, pulling back so that he could wipe away her tears.

"You do?"

"Yep. Wanna know what it is?"

She nodded.

He leaned forward and his fine mouth brushed the shell of her ear, sending hot shivers down her spine. "I want to tear off all your clothes and do bad things with you," he whispered, his voice wicked and low.

She chuckled and drew back. "For how long?"

He kissed her again, deeply. "For as long as you will let me, Bess."

"That could be a long time," she said, letting him know how she felt, how much she needed him, how much she wanted this to work.

He smiled down at her. "Good," he said. "Let's stop wasting time then, shall we?"

Starting now, Bess thought. He walked her over

to the door and she locked it, then flipped the sign to Closed. Sometimes being your own boss had distinct advantages…and this was one of them.

Epilogue

One month later...

"I REALLY LIKE HER, SON. I think she's a wonderful girl…but don't you think you're rushing things a little?"

"Yes," Lex said, looking across the backyard to his soon-to-be-bride. Sooner than any of his family actually realized, in fact. His uncle Thomas was a Baptist preacher and was going to marry them in approximately five minutes.

"And you think that's wise? You've only known her a month."

"Dad, how long had you known Mom when you knew you were going to marry her?"

His father got a faraway look in his eyes, and a slow smile dawned over his lips. He glanced up at Lex. "About two weeks," he admitted.

Lex chuckled. "Then I'm actually giving it twice

as long as you did. How long have you and Mom been married?"

"Thirty-two years."

"You want to offer me any more advice?"

"As a matter of fact, yes. She's always right. Even when she's wrong, she is right, you understand? And never let the sun go down on an argument."

Lex had only been ribbing his father, but that actually sounded like very good advice. "I love her, Dad," Lex said. "She makes me happier than I ever dreamed I could be."

"Then you're a very lucky man," his father told him.

"Ladies and gentleman," Uncle Thomas called. "Can I have your attention please?"

The crowd assembled in his parents' backyard turned, kids included, and he and Bess shared a look, then slowly made their way forward. His sister had been braiding Bess's hair and had wound little bits of baby's breath in it, making her look especially beautiful. He held out his hand and she took it.

"Now, I know y'all showed up here today thinking that you were coming to a regular old barbecue, made fine by lots of good company and good food," Thomas said. "But today we're doing something a little more special than that. Today, Lex and Bess have decided to get married and I'm officiating."

Several gasps, a few whoops and a round of applause burst through the crowd. "Lex," he heard his mother say. He turned around and saw she was patting her hair, worried over her appearance.

He winked at her, then looked back at Bess. "I love you, Bess," he said. "And I always will."

"I know you've never gotten married before, boy, but I'm supposed to tell you what to say," his uncle admonished.

The crowd laughed and tears of joy sparkled in Bess's eyes. He followed his uncle's instructions, repeated his vows, exchanged rings, then he kissed her and she became his wife.

His wife.

And nothing—nothing—had ever made him happier than hearing his uncle say, "May I now present to you Mr. and Mrs. Lex Sanborn."

She was his, Lex thought. And always would be.

* * * * *

PASSION

For a spicier, decidedly hotter read—
these are your destination for romances!

COMING NEXT MONTH
AVAILABLE NOVEMBER 22, 2011

#651 MERRY CHRISTMAS, BABY
Vicki Lewis Thompson,
Jennifer LaBrecque,
Rhonda Nelson

#652 RED-HOT SANTA
Uniformly Hot!
Tori Carrington

#653 THE MIGHTY QUINNS: KELLAN
The Mighty Quinns
Kate Hoffmann

#654 IT HAPPENED ONE CHRISTMAS
The Wrong Bed
Leslie Kelly

#655 SEXY SILENT NIGHTS
Forbidden Fantasies
Cara Summers

#656 SEX, LIES, AND MISTLETOE
Undercover Operatives
Tawny Weber

You can find more information on upcoming Harlequin® titles,
free excerpts and more at www.HarlequinInsideRomance.com.

REQUEST YOUR FREE BOOKS!
2 FREE NOVELS PLUS 2 FREE GIFTS!

ⓢHarlequin® *Blaze*™

red-hot reads!

YES! Please send me 2 FREE Harlequin® Blaze™ novels and my 2 FREE gifts (gifts are worth about $10). After receiving them, if I don't wish to receive any more books, I can return the shipping statement marked "cancel." If I don't cancel, I will receive 6 brand-new novels every month and be billed just $4.49 per book in the U.S. or $4.96 per book in Canada. That's a saving of at least 14% off the cover price. It's quite a bargain. Shipping and handling is just 50¢ per book in the U.S. and 75¢ per book in Canada.* I understand that accepting the 2 free books and gifts places me under no obligation to buy anything. I can always return a shipment and cancel at any time. Even if I never buy another book, the two free books and gifts are mine to keep forever.

151/351 HDN FEQE

Name   (PLEASE PRINT)

Address   Apt. #

City   State/Prov.   Zip/Postal Code

Signature (if under 18, a parent or guardian must sign)

Mail to the Reader Service:
IN U.S.A.: P.O. Box 1867, Buffalo, NY 14240-1867
IN CANADA: P.O. Box 609, Fort Erie, Ontario L2A 5X3

Not valid for current subscribers to Harlequin Blaze books.

Want to try two free books from another line?
Call 1-800-873-8635 or visit www.ReaderService.com.

* Terms and prices subject to change without notice. Prices do not include applicable taxes. Sales tax applicable in N.Y. Canadian residents will be charged applicable taxes. Offer not valid in Quebec. This offer is limited to one order per household. All orders subject to credit approval. Credit or debit balances in a customer's account(s) may be offset by any other outstanding balance owed by or to the customer. Please allow 4 to 6 weeks for delivery. Offer available while quantities last.

Your Privacy—The Reader Service is committed to protecting your privacy. Our Privacy Policy is available online at www.ReaderService.com or upon request from the Reader Service.

We make a portion of our mailing list available to reputable third parties that offer products we believe may interest you. If you prefer that we not exchange your name with third parties, or if you wish to clarify or modify your communication preferences, please visit us at www.ReaderService.com/consumerschoice or write to us at Reader Service Preference Service, P.O. Box 9062, Buffalo, NY 14269. Include your complete name and address.

HBI1B

*Lucy Flemming and Ross Mitchell shared a magical,
sexy Christmas weekend together six years ago.
This Christmas, history may repeat itself when they find
themselves stranded in a major snowstorm...
and alone at last.*

Read on for a sneak peek from
IT HAPPENED ONE CHRISTMAS
by Leslie Kelly.

Available December 2011, only from Harlequin® Blaze™.

EYEING THE GRAY, THICK SKY through the expansive wall of
windows, Lucy began to pack up her photography gear.
The Christmas party was winding down, only a dozen or so
people remaining on this floor, which had been transformed
from cubicles and meeting rooms to a holiday funland. She
smiled at those nearest to her, then, seeing the glances at her
silly elf hat, she reached up to tug it off her head.

Before she could do it, however, she heard a voice. A
deep, male voice—smooth and sexy, and so not Santa's.

"I appreciate you filling in on such short notice. I've
heard you do a terrific job."

Lucy didn't turn around, letting her brain process what
she was hearing. Her whole body had stiffened, the hairs on
the back of her neck standing up, her skin tightening into
tiny goose bumps. Because that voice sounded so familiar.
Impossibly familiar.

It can't be.

"It sounds like the kids had a great time."

Unable to stop herself, Lucy began to turn around,
wondering if her ears—and all her other senses—were
deceiving her. After all, six years was a long time, the mind

could play tricks. What were the odds that she'd bump into *him,* here? And today of all days. December 23.

Six years exactly. Was that really possible?

One look—and the accompanying frantic thudding of her heart—and she knew her ears and brain were working just fine. Because it was *him.*

"Oh, my God," he whispered, shocked, frozen, staring as thoroughly as she was. "Lucy?"

She nodded slowly, not taking her eyes off him, wondering why the years had made him even more attractive than ever. It didn't seem fair. Not when she'd spent the past six years thinking he must have started losing that thick, golden-brown hair, or added a spare tire to that trim, muscular form.

No.

The man was gorgeous. Truly, without-a-doubt, mouth-wateringly handsome, every bit as hot as he'd been the first time she'd laid eyes on him. She'd been twenty-two, he one year older.

They'd shared an amazing holiday season.

And had never seen one another again.

Until now.

Find out what happens in
IT HAPPENED ONE CHRISTMAS
by Leslie Kelly.
Available December 2011, only from Harlequin® Blaze™

HBEXP1211